MC ISLAND

/ / / /

J.R. RAIN

THE VAMPIRE FOR HIRE SERIES

Published by
Crop Circle Books
212 Third Crater, Moon

Copyright © 2012 by J.R. Rain

All rights reserved.

Printed in the United States of America.

ISBN-13: 978-1548323530
ISBN-10: 1548323535

Dedication
Dedicated to all the loving parents.

Acknowledgments
A special thank you to Sandy Johnston, Eve Paludan and Elaine Babich. My first readers and editors who do such a bang-up job.

"There, on our favorite seat, the silver light of the moon struck a half-reclining figure, snowy white...something dark stood behind the seat where the white figure shone, and bent over it. What it was, whether man or beast, I could not tell."
—*Bram Stoker's Dracula*

1.

"Someone killed my grandfather," said the young lady sitting in my office, "and Detective Sherbet thinks you can help me."

"I pay Detective Sherbet to say that. In donuts, of course. But not the pink ones. He has something against the pink ones."

The young girl, who was maybe twenty-five, grinned and almost clapped. "He was eating a donut when I met with him!"

"No surprise there. He's a good man."

She nodded, still grinning. A very big grin. "I got that impression, except he said there was nothing he could do for me, since my grandfather's death was ruled an accident."

"Nothing he could do," I said, "except

recommend me."

"Yes. He said I could trust you and that you would probably help, depending on your caseload."

I looked down at my desktop calendar. My mostly empty calendar. There was an appointment in three days to meet with Tammy's teacher...and that was it. The 15th was circled, which indicated that I was due a child support payment from Danny. I wasn't holding my breath—and if I had, well, I could hold it for a very long time. So far, in seven months, Danny had given me precisely one payment, and that was because I had physically hauled his ass to the bank.

"I think I can fit you in," I said. "Tell me why you think someone would want to kill your grandfather?"

"Well, I don't know."

"But you think his death is suspicious."

"Well, yes."

"When did he die?"

"A year ago."

"His death was ruled an accident?" I asked, making notes on a notepad in front of me.

"Yes."

"How did your grandfather pass away, if I may ask?"

"He was found dead in his pool."

"I'm sorry to hear that."

The young lady nodded. She reminded me of myself. Short, petite, curvy, dark hair. And unless she drank blood and hung out with other creatures of the night, that's where the resemblance ended. Her name was Tara Thurman. I seemed to have heard her name from somewhere, although I couldn't place it now.

"Where did your grandfather live?" I asked.

"On an island."

"An island?"

"Yes."

"Catalina?" I asked, which was really the only habitable island off the coast of southern California.

"No. It's in Washington State."

"I didn't know there were islands in Washington."

"There are dozens of them."

I nodded, and wondered if I had ever actually looked at a map of Washington. I didn't think so. Then again, geography was never my strong suit. Catching bad guys, now, that was a different story entirely.

"Lots of people live on the islands," she went on. "Except for my grandfather's island."

"What do you mean?"

"It's a private island. His is the only house, along with a few guest bungalows."

I thought it was time for that map. I asked her to step around my desk and show me on Google Earth where he lived. She did, leaning in next to me, smelling of perfume that I didn't recognize. She had me scroll above Seattle and—son of a bitch—there were various chains of islands scattered up there. No doubt the last Ice Age had had something to do with that, but I knew as much about ice ages as I did about maps of Washington State.

Next, she took over control of the mouse and positioned it over a speck of land above an island called Whidbey, and near another island called Lopez Island.

"I don't see it," I said.

"Hang on." She magnified the page and soon, the very small speck of land became much bigger than a speck. As it took shape, the name of the island appeared on the screen.

I looked at Tara. "You're kidding."

"About the name? No, that's what it's called."

"Skull Island?"

"Yes. I kinda like it. I used to love going there as a kid, especially telling my friends that my grandfather lived on an island called 'Skull Island.'"

"Why is it called Skull Island?"

"There was a shipwreck there a hundred or so years ago. One person died, I think. Not to mention we've unearthed a Native American burial ground. The island, I think, must have been the scene of a horrendous battle. My family has found dozens of graves."

"Sounds...creepy."

"I guess so," said Tara. "But my grandfather's home is on the other side of the island."

"Not on an Indian burial ground, I hope."

"No," she said, smiling oddly. She seemed to smile at me oddly, and often. A big smile that seemed to painfully stretch her lips. "But we do have the family mausoleum nearby."

"Excuse me?" I asked.

"The family mausoleum. The island has been in my family for nearly a century, and, well, we're all buried in the mausoleum."

"I see," I said, although I wasn't certain I did. Private islands and family mausoleums reeked of a lot of money. If I wasn't so scrupulous, my daily rates might have just increased.

Damn morals.

Tara slipped back to her seat across from my desk. As she did so, I studied her aura. It had bright yellows and greens, mixed with a pulsating thread of darkness that could have been anything. I suspected that it indicated grief.

I said, "You loved your grandfather."

She nodded and looked away. She tried to speak but instead tears suddenly burst from her eyes. I snapped out a tissue from the box on my desk, and handed it to her. She dabbed her eyes and looked away. Finally, when she'd gotten control of herself, she said, "Yes. He was so much more than a grandfather, you know? My best friend. Always there for me."

As she spoke, the dark threads of vapor that wound through her aura bulged slightly, expanding, engorging. Her grief, I suspected, ran deep.

"Do you live in Southern California?" I asked.

"Yes."

"Have you spoken to the police in Washington State?"

"No. Not yet."

"Why not use a private eye in Washington State?"

"Because Detective Sherbet recommended you."

"How do you know Sherbet?"

"He's a friend of a friend. I was told he was someone who could help."

I nodded. Something about her story wasn't jiving. And perhaps more interesting, my inner alarm began to gently ring just inside my ear. I said, "Why do you think someone killed your grandfather?"

"Because he was very rich."

"That's a reason," I said. "But that's not enough for me to take this case and to take your money. Who was there when he died?"

"We were all there."

"Who's we?"

"The entire family. We use his house and island for our annual reunion."

"You said he died a year ago."

"Right," she said, nodding. "It's coming up again. The family reunion. This weekend, in fact. And I want you to come with me."

2.

My sister and I were jogging along the boardwalk at Huntington Beach. It was midday, Saturday. My kids and her kids were with her husband at Disneyland. I wondered what her husband did to deserve such cruel and unusual punishment. I said as much to Mary Lou.

"Oh, he loves it. He's a big kid himself, you know."

"Does your husband know about me?" I asked suddenly.

Mary Lou shot me a quick look. We were both dressed in workout pants and tank tops. We both *swished* as we ran. Mary Lou's expansive upper half bounced furiously, despite her tight sports bra. Her crazily bouncing chest reminded me of two cats trying to escape a paper bag.

"Of course not," she said. "I haven't told anyone."

I nodded and frowned. I had gotten a sudden hit of her husband isolating my kids to ask them questions about me. Then again, *you* try living with a secret that could ruin you and see how suspicious you might become. A husband taking not only his own kids—but mine as well—raised some questions.

"Does he suspect anything?" I asked.

"No."

"Has he ever mentioned me?"

"Mentioned you how?"

"In a way that might make it seem like he was digging for information."

"Nothing that I can remember. C'mon, Sam. He's just doing something nice for us so that we can spend the day together. It's been so long since we could just be sisters and nothing more. And now we can spend *days* together. Glorious days. Not just nights. Okay?"

I nodded. "Okay."

But there was something here. Unfortunately, I couldn't read family members, although I could read their auras. I felt guilty as hell searching my own sister's aura to see if she was telling me the truth, but that's exactly what I did as we spoke. The verdict: I *thought* she was telling me the truth. Something suspicious had passed through her aura as she answered my questions. A ripple of sorts.

What that ripple meant, I didn't know. Reading auras was still new to me. Having psychic abilities was still new to me. Being a blood-sucking fiend...not so new to me.

I let it go. For now.

Mary Lou and I continued along the boardwalk at a steady clip. She was huffing and puffing. I don't huff or puff, although Kingsley might blow your house down. The big bad wolf that he was. Granted, I was much weaker during the day, but not so weak that I would need to stop jogging.

It was late spring and the days were growing warmer, but not so much by the beach. Mary Lou and I didn't live by the beach. We lived about ten miles inland. So a trip to the beach took planning and driving. Therefore, we planned and we drove. I probably would have preferred to sleep—okay, I most definitely would have preferred to sleep—but I could tell my sister needed some Sam time.

Hey, I was nothing if not an awesome sister.

Now Mary Lou's boobs seemed to be the main attraction on the beach. One guy stared at them for so long that he just missed running into a trash can. Mary Lou and I giggled.

These days, I could continue jogging into infinity. I was pretty sure my body didn't need to jog, that I didn't need exercise. I was pretty sure my body was a self-sustaining machine. But jogging felt...normal. It reminded me that I wasn't very far removed from the human species. I mean, I still looked human. I mostly acted human.

Mostly.

I am human, I thought. *Just...different.*

Yeah, different.

As we jogged, I told Mary Lou about my business trip this weekend, and that I would need her to watch the kids for a few days.

"They have islands in Washington?" she asked.

"That's the rumor."

"Sounds far," she said. "And cold."

"I think you and I need to buy an atlas. Or get out more."

She waved her hand at the sunny beaches. "And leave this? No thanks. Tell me about your case."

I did, easily and smoothly—and never sounded winded. Speaking as if I were sitting across from my sister at a Starbucks. Sipping water, of course. Always water.

When I finished, Mary Lou said, "Sounds dangerous. I mean, there might be a killer among them."

"Or not," I said. "My client could be delusional. The police already ruled it an accident."

"The island is isolated, right?"

I thought about that, nodding. "I think so, yeah. There's a ferry service to the island, I think."

"So, if it was isolated, perhaps the evidence had been well tampered with far before the police could come out."

"Good point," I said.

"And how long would it have taken the police to get there?"

"Another good point."

"So perhaps their assessment was wrong, or based on false information."

I looked at my sister. "You would make a good investigator."

"But a terrible vampire," she said.

I winced a little and looked around. We were alone on this segment of the boardwalk. Our shadows stretched before us. Mary Lou's shadow involved a lot of bouncing.

"Who says I'm a vampire?" I said.

She looked at me. "Still in denial, Sam? What else could you be?"

"I don't like that word vampire. I'm just...different."

She shook her head. "Whether you like that word or not, I'm pretty sure you're one, Sam. I mean, I never believed in them until you got attacked...but I sure as hell do now."

"Fine," I said. "So, why would you be a bad you-know-what?" I still couldn't say the word.

"Vampire?" she said again.

I cringed again.

She laughed and said, "Well, it's not that I would be a bad vampire. I would be a *bad* vampire, if you catch my drift."

Now I laughed. "Like an evil vampire?"

"Sure," said my sister. "I mean you can't go to hell, because you don't die. You can be as evil as you want. I think I would probably kill off most men."

"Most?"

"I would leave the pretty ones."

"Oh, brother," I said.

3.

We were on our third date.

Russell Baker was twenty-four and a professional boxer. I wasn't twenty-four. In fact, according to my driver's license, I was thirty-five. Thanks to the vampire in me, literally, I looked twenty-eight and possibly younger.

We were at Roy's Restaurant in Anaheim, a bustling place that consisted mostly of Disneyland tourist spillovers. Still, a nice restaurant with great ambiance and just enough background noise to make it seem like we were alone.

Russell Baker was dressed in tight gray jeans and wore a tight black Ralph Lauren shirt open wide at the collar, revealing some of his muscled upper chest. He wore his own type of medallion. It was a golden scorpion inside a golden disk, in homage to his birth sign. I'd heard about Scorpios. I've heard they could be the best lovers. The thought, perhaps not surprisingly, sent a shiver through me.

"You okay?" asked Russell.

"Just a little cold," I said, which was a half-truth. I was always cold. Always.

Russell seemed especially perceptive of me, and I was beginning to suspect the reason why. By our second date, I was certain he was picking up stray thoughts of mine here and there. Faster than what usually happens with most people who get close to me. After all, it had taken Detective Sherbet nearly a half a year to get to this point. Then again, Russell and I were getting close, fast.

Russell stood and plucked his light suede jacket from the back of his chair and came around the table and slipped it over my shoulders. He sat opposite me again, smooth as a jungle cat.

"Better?" he asked.

His jacket smelled of good cologne and of him, too. Essence of Russell. For me, it was a wonderfully exhilarating scent.

Despite the jacket doing nothing for me, I said, "Yes, much better." Which, again, was a half-truth. I loved his scent, and I loved his concern for me.

For me, dinner dates were a challenge. Salads were great to order for someone like me. They scattered nicely about the plate and gave the impression and appearance that I was eating my food. The wadded-up napkin in my hand contained half-masticated lettuce and carrots and beets. Anytime Russell headed for the bathroom, or checked his cell, or called over the waiter, that wadded-up napkin was gonna disappear into my purse. Lickety-split.

And so it went with me. A creature of the night —yes, a vampire, I supposed—attempting to date in the real world. Cold to the touch, unable to actually eat real food, and giving away her thoughts as if they were free.

"You're not like other girls I've dated, Sam," said Russell.

"Oh?" I wasn't exactly delighted to hear this. Lord knew I'd tried to be just like the other girls. Perhaps too hard.

And once again, I thought, *Geez, what am I doing?*

It was so much easier to be a single mom. Kingsley Fulcrum had quit calling—or trying to win me back—although I suspected I hadn't heard the last of him. Fang was gone, having disappeared with Detective Hanner, a fellow freak of the night herself. To where, I didn't know. According to Sherbet, Hanner had requested a three-month leave from the Fullerton Police Department.

Three months to turn Fang into a monster.

That thought alone turned my stomach. Then again, it could have been that stray bit of vinaigrette dressing escaping down the back of my throat. Yeah, that was gonna cause me some cramps later.

Russell was looking at me, frowning. "Who's Fang?"

My heart leaped. "Pardon?"

"You said something about a fang. I'm sorry, I'm lost."

"Oh, right," I said, thinking fast. I hadn't said anything about Fang, of course. Russell had officially picked up on my thoughts, unbeknownst to him. I said, "Oh no, I said 'dang.' As in dang this salad is good."

"You said dang and not fang?"

"Uh-huh," I said, looking away and shielding my thoughts. Too early to shield my thoughts from Russell. We were connecting—and deeply.

"Could have sworn you said something else."

"Well, it's kind of loud in here. So, you were saying I was different than the other girls?" I said, praying like hell we would change the subject.

That is, of course, if God heard my prayers.

"Right," he said, looking at me sideways a little. He then looked down at his food and played with his fork a little. Russell had very big hands, and heavily scarred knuckles. He had already told me he'd spent a childhood fighting on the streets of Long Beach. Finally, he said, "I guess it's because I feel like I can open up to you. Tell you anything."

"Is that a good thing?" I asked.

He reached across the table and took my hand. And to his credit, he didn't flinch at the cold. In fact, he never flinched at the cold. "A very good thing."

As he continued holding my hand and looking into my eyes, I think something inside me just might have melted.

I hated when that happened.

4.

The kids were at Mary Lou's and I was packing for my weekend trip when my cell rang.

"You're going on a trip," said the voice on the other end when I picked up.

I dropped my folded tank top in the suitcase. "How the devil did you know that?"

"I've been feeling it all day," said Allison. "A strong feeling that you were going away and that you needed me. I'm kinda psychic, you know. Not the full-blown type, but I think spending time with all of you vampires has sort of rubbed off on me."

I had met Allison on my last case, the girlfriend of another boxer. A murdered boxer. Allison and I had shared a...*moment*. A highly unusually moment.

Two moments, in fact, I thought.

She and I had connected, or bonded instantly. She had quickly seen through my façade, having dated a vampire herself. And the next thing I knew, she was allowing me to drink from a wound in her hand. A wound that had quickly healed once I was done drinking.

My life is so weird.

We'd talked often since, although we had yet to meet again. She had quickly become like an old girlfriend to me. A sister.

A blood sister.

"Yes, I'm going on a trip," I said, now reaching for some jeans in my closet, cradling the phone against my shoulder and ear.

"See? I knew you were going on a trip. I'm coming with you."

"No, you're not."

"Yes, I am, Sam. You need me."

"Need you how?"

"This is a business trip, no?"

"Yes, but—"

"I sense very strongly that you are going to need my help, if you know what I mean."

Actually, I did know what she meant. I stopped reaching for my jeans as I stood there in front of my open closet. A closet, I might add, that was quickly filling up with clothes. Now that I could actually go into the light of day, I needed a whole new wardrobe, right? Like that tank top I had just dropped in the suitcase. Many cute tank tops, in fact. And shorts. And sandals.

Allison was, of course, referring to fresh human blood—fresh, as in, straight from the source. A living, human source. Such blood energized me unlike anything I'd ever had before. Yes, I'd had human blood—but never hemoglobin straight from a willing source.

And Allison had been very, very willing. Apparently, she loved the experience.

I said, "I don't think my client will allow you to come."

"Say I'm your assistant."

"I doubt she'll—"

"She will, Sam. Trust me. And trust me when I say you will need me. I'm here now at the airport."

I think my mouth dropped. Correction, I know my mouth dropped open. "What airport?"

"LAX. The 4:40 flight. Lucky for me they had one seat left."

"Let me guess..." I said.

"Row 17, Seat C."

I glanced down at my ticket next to my suitcase. Row 17, Seat B."

"You're freaking me out," I said.

"I get that a lot," she said. "Now, chop-chop."

And with that, she hung up.

5.

I was halfway to LAX, fighting traffic on the 105 Freeway, when a text message came through.

Oprah had a point about not texting and driving. Oprah, as far as I knew, wasn't a vampire with cat-like reflexes and an inner alarm system that alerted me to danger.

I glanced down at my iPhone, and was not very surprised to see that it was Kingsley. Secretly—or perhaps not so secretly—I had hoped it was Fang.

Jesus, Fang...where are you?

Still, seeing the text from Kingsley warmed my heart a little. The guy was trying soooo hard to be nice. He knew he'd screwed up and screwed up royally. He also knew there was probably a very good chance I would never even see him again.

Still, he kept at it. Kept being sweet. And the big oaf was worming his way back into my life. One sweet text at a time.

Full moon tonight, his text read. *Franklin and I are gonna get our freak on.*

I shook my head and texted back: *I don't even want to begin to know what that means, goofball.*

Hey, I'll take goofball, he wrote back a few minutes later. *Better than what you've called me in the past.*

You're still a jerk.

I know. And soon I will be a hairy jerk.

Just try not to rob any graves tonight, I wrote, texting rapidly. Supernaturally fast, I might add. *That's really, really gross, by the way.*

Kingsley, as a werewolf, had a taste for corpses. That is, when and if he ever escaped the safe-room his butler Franklin locked him into each full night. A butler who was, of course, so much more than a butler.

I know, wrote Kingsley. *What's the deal with that anyway?*

In fact, I knew exactly what the *deal* with that was. Kingsley and I, although two very different creatures of the night, were not so different after all. Each of us harbored what I'd come to understand was a highly evolved dark master, an entity banned from this world, but returning through a loophole, so to speak.

And we're the loopholes.

These dark entities gave us our lives—our

eternal lives, that is—and existed within us side by side, or, if not side by side, somewhere deep within us.

I shuddered again at the thought.

And so, it was the thing within Kingsley that hungered for the flesh of the dead. And it was the thing within me that hungered for blood.

After a moment, I texted back: *I think we both know what the deal is, Wolfman. Just be a good boy tonight.*

Will do. :)

I took in a lot of air, held it in my dead lungs, and released it back into my minivan. I gripped my steering wheel and thought of Kingsley and Russell and Fang...and shook my head.

And kept on shaking it nearly all the way to LAX.

6.

We were on the plane.

"Are you hungry?" asked Allison.

"Yes, and how did you...never mind," I said, recalling her penchant for being weirdly accurate. "Yes, I am."

"You can feed from me here, if you want."

"No, I can wait," I said, embarrassed. "And I don't like the word *feed*."

"Too ghoulish?"

"Too monstrous. Not to mention it sounds like something straight out of an Anne Rice novel."

"What do you prefer?"

"Drink," I said. "I drink. Nothing more, nothing less."

"Touchy subject?" asked Allison, patting my knee condescendingly.

"Touchy life," I said.

She laughed loudly, throwing back her head, drawing attention to us. I ducked my head lower.

"Oops, sorry," said Allison, elbowing me now in the shoulder. "Most of your kind like to keep a low profile."

"My 'kind'?" I said. "Please. And could you say that a little louder?"

"Oh, I definitely could."

I grabbed her and pulled her down to my level.

"You are out of control," I said, but now I was laughing, too.

"Only seemingly, Sammie," she said, giggling, and then growing serious. "Your secret is always safe with me. Always. Except, maybe, when I'm drunk. Kidding! Hey, ouch!"

I had squeezed her forearm perhaps a little harder than I had planned. "Sorry," I said.

"No, you're not," she said, rubbing her arm. "But seriously, Sammie. Your secret is always safe."

"Then quit using words like *feed* and *your kind*. I work..." I paused, my voice faltering. For some reason, I was feeling emotional about the subject. "I work..." but my voice faltered again.

"You work hard at being normal, Sammie. I know. And when I say these words, I remind you that you're not."

We were both hunched down in our seats. I

turned and looked at her. She turned and looked at me. "That was surprisingly perceptive," I said.

"Well, you're not the first...*amazing person* I've been around."

I laughed. Allison had been the plaything for a playboy vampire who'd met his demise by the very hunter who had attacked me.

"So now I'm an amazing person?" I said.

She reached out and took my hand. Rather than flinch at the cold, she seemed to relish it, squeezing my hand even tighter and looking deeply into my eyes. "Sammie, I think you are, perhaps, the most amazing of them all."

I looked away and pulled my hand gently back. "You barely know me," I said.

"True, but I see things."

"So you say."

"And you see things, too—and you can do things others cannot."

"Other amazing people?" I said, glancing at her.

She gave me a half smile. A sad smile. "I was once connected to a very powerful vampire, Sam. Or who I had thought to be a powerful vampire. He was not as powerful as you, Sam. Not even close."

"And you know this, how?"

"I know things, remember?"

I shook my head and we both grew silent as someone walked past us down the narrow aisle. When they were gone, Allison continued, "I've always been very psychic, Sammie. In fact, I used to work at one of those psychic hotlines."

I groaned. "Oh, brother."

"Groan all you want, but I was very good. Maybe some callers thought it was a joke, but when they got on the line with me, they got the real deal." She put her hand on my forearm. "And having spent months supplying myself—giving myself to another, if you know what I mean—only amplified my gift."

I thought about that. So much to learn about myself...about what I am, and about how all of this works.

"He turned you into a super psychic," I said.

"But not just him," she said.

I glanced at her. "What do you mean?"

She held my gaze. Allison had big brown eyes. So big that, had I been able to see my own reflection, I would, no doubt, be looking at myself right now. "You, too, Sammie."

"Me, too, what?"

"When you drank from me, Sammie, you sort of re-awakened the psychic in me. And then took it to a whole new level. Which is why I think you might just be more powerful than you-know-who."

I'd heard this before, from another vampire, in fact.

"Let's change the subject," I said. "Do you mind?"

"Anything you want, Sammie."

And we did, and how we got on the subject of the Kardashians, I'll never know. But it was better than talking about me, the world's biggest freak.

The Kardashians, of course, were a whole different level of freaky.

7.

Two and half hours later, we landed at Sea-Tac Airport which, apparently, was right dab smack in the middle between Seattle and Tacoma.

"Get it?" said Allison. "Sea-Tac. As in Seattle and Tacoma."

"I get it," I said.

"Am I being annoying?" she asked.

"Not yet," I said sweetly, as we stepped out into the chilled Pacific Northwest air. "But you're getting there."

"Most of my friends say I can be annoying."

"You have honest friends," I said, keeping a straight face.

"That was rude, Samantha Moon." But she laughed anyway.

Almost immediately, a shiny Lexus SUV whipped out of the pack of circling cars and pulled up next to us. I recognized the driver. My client, Tara Thurman.

"Wow," said Allison, peeking through the passenger side window. "She looks just like her mom."

"You know her mom?" I asked as Tara stepped out. I had researched the family and knew that Tara's mother had once been a fairly well-known model, and her father was currently the vice president of the family business. A business which just so happened to be one of the biggest hotel brands in the world. A business started by the great-grandfather nearly a hundred years ago.

"Of course," said Allison. "Everyone knows of her mom. At least, everyone down at the shop."

I wasn't sure which "shop" she was referring to, and before I could ask, Tara was already coming toward us. She certainly did not inherit her mother's stature nor build. Like I said, she was shaped more like me. Short and a little curvy.

Earlier, Tara had agreed to allow Allison to join me as my assistant. I was certain she wouldn't agree, but Allison had seemed confident that Tara would. To my surprise, my client had indeed agreed, telling me that, although these yearly reunions were generally for family, sometimes friends or significant others did join in.

I introduced the two, and we all climbed in. I took the front seat and Allison the back, and as the

SUV pulled away, Allison leaned forward through the seats and said, "So, is the Space Needle really a needle?"

"Okay," I said. "*Now* you're being annoying."

***

As the 5 Freeway wended and twisted its way through the tree-lined suburbs outside of Seattle, Tara, Allison and I had a crash course in friendship.

According to Tara, no one was to know that I was a private eye, or that Allison was my assistant. This wasn't a murder investigation. Not officially. This was a family reunion, on a remote island, during which I would pretend to be a friend, although I would be secretly snooping my ass off.

Luckily, I'm damn good at snooping my ass off.

We decided to give me a fake name, too. After all, it wouldn't do having a nosy family member Googling my name and finding my agency's website. So, we decided that being old college chums was best, chums who'd recently met again in Seattle and were only now catching up. Allison was my visiting friend, who got invited along for the weekend getaway.

So, we spent the remainder of the time in the SUV boning up on Tara's college. It turned out she'd gone to UCLA, and graduated with a degree in psychology. I was going to pretend to be a college dropout. Allison pointed out that someone with enough snooping skills could verify that I, in fact, never went to UCLA. So, we decided to give me a very generic name.

Samantha Smith.

In fact, being *Samantha Smith* for a three-day weekend might just be a welcome relief.

And maybe a little fun.

Especially as we approached the glittering emerald city, whose skyline matched the beauty of any skyline anywhere, and as we did, I received a text message from my son.

Tammy's reading my mind again, Mom.

I sighed and dashed off a quick text to my daughter: *Quit reading your brother's mind, booger butt. And make sure you do your homework.*

8.

The drive through Seattle was far too quick.

Admittedly, I wanted to stay and explore. The Space Needle, to Allison's dismay, was not a needle, but an orange-topped, UFO-shaped disc that looked less like a needle and more like a giant alien probe.

Still, the city was brilliantly lit, packed with nice cars, and restaurants seemingly everywhere. I could see why Frasier would want to live here. A light rain was falling, which, from what I understood, was as common as sunshine in southern California.

Vampire weather, I thought.

Soon we were eating up the miles north of Seattle, while Tara and I continued to hash out our fake history together. We created parties we never went to, the names of boys we never met, and classes we never took together. A fake history. An iron-clad history. Allison quizzed us as we drove through a city called Mukilteo—a name I never did seem to pronounce correctly—and drove onto a ferry with service to an island called Whidbey.

"We're in the car," said Allison, sticking her head out the window, "but we're on a boat, too." She sounded perplexed.

"Yes," said Tara, looking at me and giving me a half smile. "A ferry, actually."

"A car on a boat," Allison said again, shaking her head. "What will they think of next?"

"You've never been on a ferry before?" asked Tara.

"I've never been on a *boat* before," said Allison. "Do these ferries ever sink?"

"Often," said Tara.

Allison pulled her head out of the window. Her reddish cheeks had quickly drained to white. "How often do they—wait, you're messing with me."

"Sorry," said Tara, giggling a little from behind the wheel. She winked at me. "I couldn't resist. My bad."

"No worries," said Allison. "I'm a kidder, too. Must run in our family."

"Excuse me?" asked Tara. "Family?"

Allison popped her gum. "Yup. We're like eleven cousins removed."

"Oh, really?" said Tara.

"Yup, I'm also distantly related to Bill Clinton

and Barack Obama. Genealogy is a passion of mine."

I rolled my eyes. Tara smiled, uncomfortably.

Allison went back to sticking her head out the window, the way a dog might, as the ferry continued across the Puget Sound. The waves were choppy, but the ferry handled them with aplomb. We were in a long row of cars, many of which were filled with tired-looking men and women, all dressed nice, and all clearly returning home from work on the mainland.

When the ferry docked in a city called Clinton —and once Allison had taken her seat like a good girl—we followed the long line of cars off the ferry and onto the island.

A gorgeous island, no less.

"There's trees everywhere," said Allison. "And I mean some big-ass trees."

I was suitably impressed, as well, and after we stopped at a cute little coffee kiosk—at which I politely declined a cup—we continued north up the island, wending and winding our way through endless trees, stretches of beaches and luscious farmlands.

The drizzle of rain followed us, but there was no traffic on this island. Just a few well-spaced homes, a few well-spaced cars, endless greenery...and a delightful lack of sun.

We passed cities called Freeland and Greenbank and a bigger town called Oak Harbor. Up we went over a majestic bridge called Deception Pass that made even my mouth drop. Allison *ohed* and *ahed*, and Tara seemed genuinely pleased to see our stunned responses. The bridge apparently connected one island to another, and arched high above roiling currents.

I felt almost as if I had taken flight, so high were we above the foaming waters below.

The bridge came and went much too quickly for my taste, as we wound our way ever north to another charming town called Anacortes where we parked the SUV and boarded a smaller boat.

Smaller, but not by much.

9.

I was standing near the prow, doing my best not to lift my arms and shout that I was the Queen of the World. Or, perhaps more accurately, Queen of the Underworld.

I stood there, holding onto a post, and stared out at the rolling sea. Heavy fog hung low over the water. The sea itself was slate gray and seemingly impenetrable. At the most, I could see down only a few feet. Nothing seemed to exist near the surface. No dolphins nor seals nor killer whales. The Puget Sound seemed devoid of life. Just a vast expanse of churning, dead, gray water, a barrier between islands. A great moat, perhaps.

Which didn't make it any less beautiful. On the contrary, I lived a dozen or so miles from the ocean, so it wasn't often that I found myself bouncing along a fast-moving boat, through a heavy fog, hundreds of feet above the ocean floor.

Tara was sitting with the captain, and Allison was below deck, battling seasickness and failing miserably. Last I heard, she was introducing herself to the tiny metal toilet attached to the main sleeping quarters below deck. The boat itself sported a bedroom, a living room, and a galley. The boat was cozy and was captained by a smallish man with a biggish beard. He could have been Ahab in another life. Or perhaps even the white whale.

With that thought, I thought of Ishmael. No, not the Ishmael from *Moby Dick*. Ishmael who had been, at one time, my guardian angel. And who was now...I didn't know.

An interested suitor? Maybe, maybe not.

I didn't know much, but I did know one thing: *my life was weird.*

Sometimes too weird.

Sometimes I wanted to bury my head in the sand, or leap, say, from this boat, and drift to the ocean floor and exist in silence and peace, with the crabs and bottom feeders. Except I couldn't run away from what I was, or what my children had become. What they had become because of me.

Suddenly, panic and dread and a crushing fear filled me all over again.

Breathe, Samantha.

I did so now—slowly, deeply, filling my useless lungs to capacity with air that I didn't need—at least, not in the physical sense. Emotionally, maybe.

As I focused on my breathing, as the cold air flowed in and out of my lungs, in and out of my nostrils, I had the distinct sensation of being out of my body. I hadn't planned to be—who planned that sort of thing, anyway?—and hadn't even expected it. One moment, I was concentrating on keeping calm, focused almost entirely on the process of breathing, and the next...

The next, I was...elsewhere.

Not literally, for I could hear the roar of the boat's motors, the wind thundering over my ears, the water slapping against the hull. Yes, I could feel and hear and smell, but I was not there. Not in the boat.

Then again, maybe I really was nuts and was sitting in some insane asylum. Maybe the doctors had just given me my latest dose of zone-out meds.

Do not be so hard on yourself, Samantha Moon.

Was that my voice? Had I made it up? I wasn't certain. I did know that the sound of the ocean and the boat and the wind seemed to be fading even further away. Although I felt detached from my body—hell, from reality—the voice was, to say the least, a welcome sensation.

Very good, Samantha Moon.

The thought was not my own, I was certain of it.

No, not so much a thought as a *voice* whispered just inside my ear. I was very familiar with such telepathic communication...but this communication seemed different somehow. It almost seemed to come from inside of me—and around me and through me, all at the same time.

A good way of looking at our communication, Sam.

I was also certain I'd heard the voice before, as I'd sat upon a desert ledge, back when I'd let my mind drift and found myself in a deeply meditative state—and in the presence of something very loving.

And seemingly all-knowing.

All-loving, Samantha Moon.

I continued holding onto the post as my knees absorbed the rising and falling of the boat. But I wasn't on the ship. No, not really. I was elsewhere. Above my body. In a place nearby but not nearby. I struggled for words, searching for an explanation to where I was. To what was happening to me.

Let's call it a frequency, Samantha. You are in a higher frequency.

I don't understand.

You will, someday.

The boat dipped deeply, no doubt plunging into a trough, but I effortlessly kept my footing, my balance. Even in a deeply meditative state, my uncanny reflexes were working overtime.

In my mind's eye, I saw myself standing before something big. No, not just something big. The biggest. The biggest of all. The Universe, perhaps. There was movement, too. Planets were rotating. No, not just planets. Whole solar systems, galaxies and universes were rotating. I saw stars being born and destroyed. I saw whole universes collapsing and birthing. The Universe was alive to my eyes, as surely as if I was watching a hive of bees at work.

I was certain that I was watching the Universe from the perspective of something much greater than me.

You are seeing it through yourself, Samantha.

No, I thought, and felt myself shaking my head back on the boat. *I am seeing it through God. The eyes of God.*

Correct, Samantha.

How I saw this, I didn't know, where I was, I didn't know. I seemed outside of space and time, all while standing here on the boat's prow, cutting through the fog and mist and now a light drizzle upon the Puget Sound.

But you said I was seeing it through my eyes, I asked the voice in my head. The voice that I was beginning to think was God.

Correct again.

I don't understand.

Yes, you do, Samantha.

Perhaps I did know. I'd heard the voice all my life but had never really understood it. Until now.

It's because I'm a part of you, too, I thought.

Very good, Samantha.

I was next given a glimpse of something that had never occurred to me before, not until now. *I'm not just a part of you,* I thought, *but you are me.*

Very good, Sam.

I am you, experiencing life.

Very true, Samantha. As are all people, all things.

But, why? I asked. *You are God, why experience life through me? I am nothing. I am a blip in the universe. All of us are blips.*

And what if you had access to the sum total of all blips, Samantha? Billions and billions of blips?

I would have access to, well everything.

Indeed, Samantha Moon.

Why are you talking to me now? I asked.

Because you are much more than a blip, Samantha.

And now I saw, through another glimpse—or perhaps this was an epiphany—that I was no greater or smaller than others in our world. But because of who I am, or what I was, I had an open channel to God. To the universe. To the spirit world in general.

You're talking to me now because I can hear you, I said.

No, Sam. I'm talking to you now because you are listening.

Footsteps slapped behind me, and I snapped back into my body and gasped when I saw the captain swing down below deck. He saw me and nodded and, although I tried to smile back, all I could see were worlds being destroyed.

And worlds being born.

10.

"You look like you've seen a ghost," said Allison. "And, for you, that's saying something."

"Gee, thanks," I said.

But the truth was, I had seen a ghost.

Not a ghost, I thought. *God.*

I shook my head again. The boat had docked along a floating pier. The three crew members were busy securing the vessel, using a system of ropes and, apparently, rubber tires that acted as buffers between the hull and the wooden pier. All of it seemed more complex than I could comprehend. Especially considering my mind—or soul—had been far elsewhere.

To the far edges of the universe, in fact.

Lordy, my life is weird.

Allison wasn't looking too swell herself. In fact, she looked, I suspected, as pale as myself. Why I still looked pale these days, I didn't know. After all, thanks to the medallion that seemed to be permanently embedded just beneath my skin, I'd been able to head out into the sun for the past few months now. Glorious months.

You're pale, I thought, as I reluctantly accepted the hand of one of the shipmates who helped me across the gangplank, *because you're dead.*

I didn't feel dead, of course. I felt alive. And, when the sun went down, more alive than I'd ever felt in my life. Ever.

Once on the pier, as we followed Tara and a few other passengers—passengers that Tara knew and who were, I suspected, relatives—Allison caught up to me.

"Seriously, Sam, what's wrong?" she whispered in my ear. I couldn't help but notice her breath smelled of vomit. Blech. "You look...out of it."

"I'll tell you about it later," I said over my shoulder.

She was about to fall back behind me when her eyes suddenly widened. "God?" she said, obviously reading my thoughts—thoughts that I had left open to her. "You talked to God? Seriously?"

"If not, then a heck of an imposter."

"So weird."

"Tell me about it."

And with that, Allison turned her head and just

made it to the edge of the pier before she heaved what little remained in her stomach.

***

"As you can see, this is a private island," explained Tara Thurman.

She was driving behind a motorcade of Range Rovers. There were three in total, including our own. The road wasn't paved, but it was the next best thing—smooth. Allison seemed to appreciate the smooth part, although she was still looking a little green.

"I feel green," she whispered to me, reading my thoughts.

Our strong connection was surprising even me. I suspected that, coupled with her own psychic intuition, our telepathic link was particularly sensitive, thanks to the exchange in blood.

"You bet your britches," she said.

"Will you quit doing that?" I whispered to her.

"Excuse me?" said Tara from behind the wheel.

"Oh, nothing," I said, mentally pushing Allison out of my thoughts. "You were saying about the island?"

Tara, who was focused on the dirt road and the caravan in front of us, hardly seemed to notice this particular conversation between Allison and me. Instead, she nodded, clearly proud of the island.

"Like I said, the island has been in my family for nearly one hundred years. It was first purchased by my great-grandfather, who built the home. My grandfather inherited it, and spent the last thirty years of his life here. The rest of us have used the island on and off for vacations and getaways and reunions."

I nodded. We were surrounded by massive evergreens, each rising high above the car windows, effectively blocking out the sun, which I was always thankful for. Yes, although I existed somewhat comfortably in the light of day, I always appreciated deep shade.

Must be the ghoul in me.

The island itself seemed to be primarily surrounded by cliffs and bluffs. So far, the only sandy beach had been where the boat had docked, where the row of Range Rovers had been waiting.

"Are there any bears on the island?" asked Allison from the back, poking her head between the front seats.

Tara laughed. "No bears or predators of any kind on the island. We have deer and raccoons and squirrels and a few resident seals that prefer the rocks along the north part of the island."

The road shifted inland, cutting through a narrow road that seemed to barely have enough room for the bigger vehicles. Tara drove comfortably, clearly used to this scenic drive. Branches occasionally slapped the fender and roof.

"We have food and supplies shipped daily from the mainland. There's a courier service we use. Not to mention any of us who come over from the mainland bring additional supplies."

"Sounds kinda...fun," said Allison.

"Heaven, if you ask me. My grandfather was always so open to all of us. What he had, we had. He held nothing back and always made everyone feel so welcome." As she spoke these words, her lips curled up into that curious smile again.

So weird, I thought.

I also couldn't help but to notice the sadness in her voice. Her grandfather had been found, of course, face-down in a swimming pool. Allison seemed to detect Tara's tone as well and sat back in her seat. We were somber and quiet for the rest of the drive.

And what a drive it was. Winding roads, beautiful greenery, squirrels and rabbits...and then, finally, the road opened into a massive estate.

Where there had once been forest was now, perhaps, the most beautiful home I had ever seen.

"Sweet mama," said Allison.

11.

We pulled around a curved, brick, herringbone driveway.

The house, I think, was even bigger than Kingsley's monster of a house—Beast Manor, as I'd come to think of his home, complete with its safe-room.

This house was epic and rambling on a whole other level, and I was fairly certain there was even more of it in the back, too. Tara explained that the design was a Mediterranean-style Spanish Revival. Having minored in architecture in college—with a major in criminal justice—I knew the design well. But seeing it up close, and in such grandeur, was awe-inspiring.

I could be very comfortable here, I thought. *A*

home fit for a king. Even a vampire queen.

Allison was still oh-ing and ah-ing as we stepped out of the Range Rover. I might have *oh-ed*, but I certainly hadn't *ah-ed*. The house itself was situated on lushly manicured grounds, complete with sumptuous gardens filled, in part, with fresh herbs. I saw everything from sage to rosemary, to mint and thyme. The home's courtyard had a distinctively European flair, with intricate brick and plasterwork. Trees were the overall theme of the home and sprouted from ornate planters situated everywhere. A five-car garage was off to one side. The garage and much of the home's façade was covered in thick ivy.

"I'm in heaven, Sammie," said Allison. "Remind me to thank you again for inviting me to join you."

"I didn't invite you. You insisted."

"And I'm so glad I did."

I shook my head as we each fetched our suitcases from the rear of the vehicle. As we headed up the wide flagstone stairs, I noticed Tara, our host, looking at me. Or, rather, at my suitcase.

"You don't roll your bag?" she asked.

Oops. My bag, I saw, was bigger than both Tara's and Allison's. And both of them were struggling a bit up the steps, rolling and lifting. I had mine in my hand, hefting it without thought or effort. "I like the exercise," I lied. "My trainer would be proud."

Tara smiled as if I had made some sense.

Allison snickered behind me. And once we were inside the cavernous home, I acted normal and used my suitcase's own rollers.

The home opened onto two curving staircases with ornate, wrought-iron railings. Polished wood floors stretched seemingly everywhere. A beautiful, round marble table with fresh-cut flowers in a crystal vase greeted us immediately, along with the sound of laughter and voices and kids playing.

"Grandpa George—that's what everyone called him, even his wife—never made any of us feel unwelcome. The entire house was *on-limits*, as he would always say."

"On-limits?" asked Allison. She was scurrying to keep up behind us. Turned out my new friend had rather short legs.

I heard that, she thought, her words reaching me easily.

I giggled.

I heard that, too. And yes, I have issues with my legs.

I stopped giggling, or tried to.

"Well," said Tara, speaking over her shoulder as we headed into a gorgeous living room. "Grandpa George always told us the entire house was available to all of us kids. There was never a room we were not allowed in, except—"

She paused.

"Except what?" I asked.

"Well, the family mausoleum, of course."

"Er, of course," I said. "Grandpa George sounds

like he was an amazing man."

Tara nodded and tensed her shoulders. "Yeah, the best."

We next passed through the kitchen, where three or four people were leaning against counters, drinking and talking. Tara said hi and introduced us as her friends. They all smiled and raised their drinks, but watched us closely. Very closely. It was the same for the other rooms and other people. Introductions, polite smiles, suspicious stares.

As we swept through the house and out through a pair of wide French doors, Allison caught up to me on her stubby legs and whispered in my ear, "What was that all about?"

"What do you mean?"

"The stares. Creepy."

"I don't know," I said.

"At least not yet," said Allison.

"Right," I said, as we now followed Tara along a curved, stone path that led through even more succulent gardens. There was a volleyball net set up out here, along with kayaks lined along an arbor with what was, perhaps, the biggest brick barbeque I'd ever seen. The home, I was beginning to realize, was designed for one thing and one thing only: pleasure, and lots of it. At least of the family kind. A sort of funhouse for adults and kids and everyone in between.

"But we're going to find out," said Allison.

"I'm going to find out," I corrected.

"Hey, I'm your assistant."

"Fictional assistant," I added.

And there it was, just around another turn in the path: the swimming pool where Tara's grandpa had been found last summer, face down and quite dead. I noticed Tara kept her eyes averted. I didn't blame her.

Next, was a row of guest homes in the back, which is where Allison and I would be staying. Bungalows, actually. Each was as big or bigger than my home in Fullerton. Tara showed us to one such structure, which proved to be a two-bedroom suite, with bedrooms on either end and a kitchen and living room in the middle. A fireplace was there, too. Firewood and kindling was stacked neatly nearby.

I made arrangements with Tara to come back and debrief us once we were unpacked and settled in. I also requested that she bring family photos. I needed to know everyone who was here. Intimately. She understood.

"Debrief?" asked Allison when Tara had left.

"That's detective talk," I said.

"You mean detective mumbo-jumbo."

"Remember why we're here," I said. "To catch a killer."

"Well, I'm here to keep you alive."

I snorted.

"Don't scoff," said Allison. "I saw it clearly."

"You saw what clearly?"

"Me saving your life."

"How?"

"I'm not sure yet."

"Convenient."

"Don't scoff at us mystics, Sammie. We work in mysterious ways."

I snorted again and picked the room on the left.

"Hey," said Allison. "Why do you get that room?"

"Because you work for me, remember?"

"Oh, damn," said Allison, plopping down on her own bed and then stretching out. "I forgot about that part."

But she was asleep before I could respond.

12.

Yes, I wanted to sleep, too.

And, yes, the medallion made it possible for me to withstand the sun, but the golden disk didn't take away the *burning desire* to lay down, close my eyes, and die all over again. Because that's how sleep often felt to me: a mini-death.

I am so very, very weird.

But I was also here only for the weekend. It was Friday afternoon, and coming on evening. I had tonight, tomorrow and all of Sunday to solve this crime. Our flight back to civilization was Monday morning.

Lots to do, I thought. *Too much to be laying around and snoozing.*

I pulled out the one thing every good

investigator needs: my clipboard with my case notes. Yes, I'd already been making notes on this one. Lots of them. Knowing I had only a few days to prep for this case meant that I needed names and pictures. I looked at my list now of the many names, some of which had thumbnail pictures next to them. I had drawn lines attaching the names to various family members.

For now, they were just names and pictures and slightly squiggly lines. The deceased in question was George Thurman, or Grandpa George. The name had a certain ring to it. Yes, he sounded important but—but from what I was gathering, he didn't act it. He was a recluse at heart who loved his family. Although he was known for his generosity to charities, he rarely, if ever, opened up his home to outsiders.

His home was his safe haven, his escape.

And now, his tomb.

George Thurman had had two sons and a daughter, all of whom now ran the family hotel empire. An empire that was very much kept in the family. Much like his home, where only family members were invited, the business was the same: only family members were appointed to important roles. For now, it was the eldest son, Junior Thurman, who was the president. The youngest son, August, was the vice-president. Other important roles went to brothers and sisters, uncles and aunts, nephews and nieces. George's wife, Ellery, had long since passed.

By all accounts, the family was über-rich. The two sons' own daughters were often found in tabloid magazines. One of them had even made a sex tape. I'd refused to watch the sex tape. For now. Yes, I knew I needed to be thorough...but *eww*.

From the next room, I heard Allison mumble something in her sleep. The mumbling then turned into loud snoring. I got up and shut her bedroom door, just as she let out a short, sharp snort.

Nice.

Back in the living room, I looked some more at my notes. The deceased in question, George Thurman, had long since retired, handing the corporate over to his oldest son. That had been, according to my research, nearly ten years ago. So, power couldn't have been a factor.

Money, maybe.

Undoubtedly, George had left untold millions behind, bequeathing them to who knows who. The potential to inherit millions of dollars might be a motivating factor.

But to sons who were already wealthy?

That didn't ring true.

I made a note to follow up on the disbursement of the inheritance, who got what and how much. But I suspected this was a dead end. Then again, what did I know? As for me, the most I could leave my own kids was a mortgage in which I was almost upside down. That and a minivan and, maybe, a few thousand dollars in petty cash.

I need to get my shit together, I thought.

I went back to what I knew of George Thurman's death. As I did so, I got up from the leather couch and moved over to the front door, where I stood in the doorway and looked out across the manicured grounds. There were four bungalows, and untold numbers of guest rooms in the mansion. Enough, surely, for twenty or thirty people to stay comfortably.

There was the pool behind the main house. There was a fence around the pool, which was a good idea with all the grandkids. There was also a balcony directly above the pool, a balcony that led off to one of the rooms.

Had he been pushed? Had he fallen in?

According to the autopsy, there had been no alcohol in the old man's system, nor any drugs. George hadn't had a heart attack, either, nor a stroke. In fact, there had been no evidence of foul play of any type. His death had been ruled an accidental drowning.

George Thurman had been 79 at the time of his death. Too old to remember how to swim? Hell, how does one accidentally drown, anyway?

I didn't know as I gazed out over the sun-drenched backyard, as the shadows of evening encroached.

Time to get to work.

13.

Allison was still asleep.

I could smell the barbeque cooking. The smoking meat triggered a primal hunger in me, a hunger that I couldn't feed. I hadn't brought any of my own *nourishment* with me. Allison had volunteered for the job. Fresh blood. *Her* blood. Smelling the meat now triggered a hunger in me.

A hunger for *her*.

Jesus.

I found myself pacing inside the small bungalow. The floorboard creaked beneath me. I always paced at this time of the day, medallion or no medallion. When the sun was about to set, that thing which was inside me awakened.

Awakened to the night.

I paused at the open window. The sky beyond was purplish—and filling up with low-hanging clouds. So much for the sunny skies. This was, after all, the Pacific Northwest.

And just like that, the first drops appeared against the big window, splattering, collecting, sliding.

I continued pacing.

As I paced, both a sadness and an excitement filled me. Excitement for the coming night. Sadness for what I was. After all, just when I would think I was feeling normal, or feeling human, this would happen: the day would merge into night. And, when that happened, I would feel anything but normal. Anyone but myself.

I felt on edge, anxious, angry.

This would be when I would snap at Tammy and Anthony—and even more often at Danny—more than enough times for them to know to stay away from Mommy at this time of day. Of course, back in the day, my kids didn't know the reason why.

Now they did. Now they knew everything.

They knew Mommy was a freak. They also knew that they were pretty freaky themselves.

Not my fault, I thought, as I shook my hands and continued pacing. *I didn't ask for this. I was only out jogging. Jogging as I had done many times before. Hundreds of times before.*

Had the bastard been watching me seven years ago? Or had I simply crossed paths with him unexpectedly? An unfortunate crossing of paths?

I didn't know...and perhaps would never know, unless...

Unless I talked to the vampire hunter who'd killed my own attacker. The vampire hunter named Rand.

Then again, wasn't there another who knew the answers? My guardian angel had been neither a guardian nor an angel.

Ishmael had, apparently, orchestrated my attack. How, I didn't know, but I was going to find out. What strings had he pulled? In the least, what did the son-of-a-bitch know?

I shook my hands again.

Good God, when was the fucking sun going to set?

Soon, I knew. Soon. I could feel it out there, beyond the forest of evergreens. Its rounded upper half was still above the distant horizon. I couldn't see it but I could *feel* it. Every ray. Every particle of light. Every fucking photon.

Screw Fang. He didn't have to push me so hard. I might have come around. I might have fallen in love with him, too. Screw Detective Hanner, too. Whatever her game was, I didn't know, but I did know one thing.

She wasn't going to win. Not if she came up against me.

And by stealing Fang from me—my very best friend—well, she made it personal. Very, very personal.

I accidentally elbowed the corner of the kitchen. Plaster exploded and the whole house shook.

Easy, I thought. *Calm down.*

I thought of Danny and Kingsley. Two cheaters. Two bastards, and I nearly drove my hand through the front door as I passed by it.

That's not calming down, I thought.

I thought of my kids and took a deep breath. I thought of Detective Sherbet and smiled. I thought of Allison snoring in the room next to me, and almost laughed.

I was calming down. Good. Willing myself to calm down. Yes, good. But there was another reason for why I was finally relaxing. Oh, yes, another reason, indeed.

The sun was slip, slip, slippin' away.

I paused by the big window and breathed in deeply, filling my worthless lungs to capacity with useless air. And by the time I had filled them completely, the anger and hostility had disappeared.

I felt like a new woman. Or a new vampire.

The sun, after all, had set.

And I was alive again.

Truly alive.

I turned around and saw Allison watching me from the shadows of her doorway, her hair mussed. "Feeling better?" she asked.

"Very," I said.

"Hungry?"

"Very, very hungry," I said.

14.

Dinner was served in the dining room.

And what a dining room it was. It had a vaulted ceiling complete with a hand-painted mural of a mountain that I suspected was the nearby Mount Rainier. Very Sistine Chapel-like, and it, no doubt, would have taken a skilled artisan months to complete. The dining table itself looked like it was out of a movie set. So long that it seemed comical, it was vaguely boat-shaped, as in, it tapered off near the end, wider in the middle. It had a beautiful golden floral inlay, with intricately carved pedestals holding the whole damn thing steady.

Italian, I figured, and worth more money than I would make in a month. *Two months.*

Steaming filet mignon and crusted chicken

breasts and barbequed ribs filled many platters placed along the center of the table. All of which smelled heavenly. All of which were off-limits to me. Yes, I accepted a small serving of salad, claiming I was a vegetarian. Allison snickered at that, and I gave her a small elbow in the ribs.

Well, maybe, not that small. She *oophed* and nearly toppled over.

My bad, I thought.

Meanie, she thought back.

But she had played it off well, turning the explosion of air into a hacking cough that earned a few scowls from those around the table. When she was done hacking into her napkin, she glared at me. I shrugged and smiled sweetly.

I counted seventeen people in all. Thirteen adults and four kids. The kids ranged from tweens to toddlers. Tara sat on the other side of me. I recognized the man at the head of the table: George Thurman Junior. Or, as he preferred, Junior, according to Tara who'd gotten Allison and I caught up, just before dinner. Patricia Thurman, Junior's beautiful wife—too beautiful and too perfect, if you asked me—sat to his right and didn't stop looking at me.

There was an older couple sitting together across from me. They both smiled warmly at me. There was a devilishly handsome young man who hadn't stopped staring at Allison. To her credit, remarkably, she'd ignored him completely. I knew she was still grieving for her one-time boyfriend, the boxer, Caesar Marquez, and wasn't in the market for men. There were two men sitting together, rather closely. I caught them smiling warmly at each other. Next to Tara was a young man who looked oddly familiar. No, not familiar. I mean, yes, I'd seen his picture before, but there was something about him...

Then I figured it out. His smile. It was the same kind of big, expressive smile that I had seen on Tara, my client. Lips curled up. Almost clown-like.

His name was Edwin Thurman, and he was Junior's only son, the black sheep of the family with a history of drugs, public arrests and jail time.

I scanned the entire lot. Yes, a psychic scan of sorts. I couldn't read everyone's mind, thank God. Yes, it turned out that I could actually influence thoughts. But I could also get impressions from people. I noted, in particular, that my inner alarm was ringing mildly. There was a potential threat here, somewhere at the table.

I hated when that happened.

Dinner was served. There was no wait staff, which I found slightly curious. A big house like this with no staff? Who cleaned and cooked and manicured the lawns?

So, we served ourselves, like commoners. Of course, I just picked at my salad and scattered it around and pretended to eat, all while I spat it back in my napkin. I drank the wine, which at least gave me some semblance of humanity.

The dinner was mostly subdued. No one asked

any questions of Allison or me. No one really looked our way. No one, except for Junior's beautiful wife. The kids talked quietly among themselves, often laughing.

The many couples talked quietly, too. I scattered the salad sufficiently and Allison, bless her heart, reached over and picked at my salad as well. The end result was that I appeared to have eaten my light dinner, or at least some of it. I appeared, for all intents and purposes, to be one of the living.

As I pushed my salad away, feigning fullness, the young man sitting next to Allison looked at it, then at my nearly finished goblet of wine.

And smiled at me.

Knowingly.

15.

We retired to the great room.

Yes, *retired.* That's how Junior Thurman phrased it. I'm fairly certain I'd never retired to any room, let alone a great room. But, if sitting in comfy chairs and holding my wine and trying to pretend to be normal was retiring, then there was a first for everything.

As we sat, I sent a thought over to Allison for her to shield her own thoughts. She asked why and I told her to just do it, that I would explain later. She shrugged, and I sensed her mind closing to me, exactly the way I had taught her to do it.

Good girl, I thought, although she wouldn't be able to hear me.

The great room was, well, great. It had a soaring

ceiling crisscrossed with thick beams. It had arches and a brick fireplace and oversized furniture. The room was something to behold. And, apparently, to retire in.

Outside, through the stacked windows framed with heavy curtains, the tall evergreens were now swaying violently, although I doubted the others could see them in the darkness. A storm was moving in. A big one, too.

"It's getting blustery out there," said Edwin, the young man who might have been handsome if not for the perpetual smile on his face. He could see the trees as well?

"Blustery?" said Allison next to me. She'd had two glasses of wine. She was also smaller than me and hadn't eaten much at dinner. I suspected the wine had gone straight to her head.

Junior Thurman, who'd been texting on his too-big cell phone, set it aside and looked up at her. He was holding a glass of sherry. I was fairly certain I'd never before seen anyone drink a glass of sherry in my life.

Another first, I thought.

"It's a word we like to use up here," he said jovially enough. He had a strong, resonant voice that seemed to fill the great room. His wife nodded. She had quit looking at me. Now she was staring down into her own glass of wine, legs tucked under her.

Junior went on: "Blustery is just our way saying that we're getting some nasty weather out there, nasty even for the Northwest."

"We just call it a shit-storm where I'm from," said Allison, and immediately looked like she regretted it.

The kids who'd been playing cards nearby looked up. Junior frowned a little. Edwin, I saw, grinned even bigger.

"And where are you from, Allison?" Junior asked pleasantly.

"Texas."

"Ah," said Junior without elaborating, as if that answered everything. He turned his attention back to me. "Samantha, from where do you know my dear niece?"

"I've known Tari since we were in college," I said, reciting the script. Tara was "Tari" to friends and family.

Junior nodded. He held the glass of sherry loosely in his hands. The rich vermillion color caught some of the ambient light. From here, the liquid looked like blood. My stomach growled. My sick, ghoulish stomach.

He said, "Did you two have many classes together?"

"One or two," I said, "until I dropped out."

"And why would you do a thing like that?" asked Patricia, Junior's wife.

"I got pregnant," I lied.

"Twins," said Allison, jumping in.

Junior nodded, as if that made perfect sense. I nearly frowned at Allison. We hadn't discussed me having twins. She'd drunkenly embellished the story. Tara was looking concerned, too.

"Twins," said Mrs. Thurman. "How delightful. What are their names?"

"Tammy and Anthony."

"They're not, you know, identical," said Allison, slurring her words slightly.

Mrs. Thurman regarded Allison curiously. "I gathered that." She turned back to me. "And you've kept in touch with our Tari all this time?"

"On and off," I said, lying easily. It was, after all, what investigators did. We often lied to get our information.

"We reconnected through Facebook," blurted Allison.

"Oh, so you're friends on Facebook?" asked Edwin. He continued smiling. He seemed to be getting a kick out of all of this.

I saw where this was going, and saw where Allison had screwed up. I said, "I don't think so, not yet. We just emailed."

Edwin leaned forward and rested his elbows on his knees and looked directly at me. His face was angular, his cheekbones high. His lips were a little too full, even for me. He said, "Maybe we can be friends on Facebook."

"Maybe," I said. "Depends how friendly you are."

He laughed and sat back.

"I just love Facebook," said Allison. "Just last week a friend of mine sent me this cat video...I swear to God that little booger was clapping. Clapping! A kitten! Can you believe it?"

Apparently, no one could. Or they were too dumbfounded to speak. Junior shifted his considerable gaze from me to her. The president of Thurman Hotels was also, apparently, the leader of the family, too. "And how do you know our Tari?"

"Oh, I'm just here for the ride," said Allison, sitting back and kicking her Uggs comfortably. She snapped her gum. "I'm with Sammie here. Where she goes, I go."

"Cute," said Patricia.

Time to change the subject. "This is a beautiful home," I said.

The older couple sitting near the roaring fireplace sat forward. Elaine Thurman, sister of the deceased. She smiled brightly. Her aura, I saw, was bluish and yellow, which told me she was a woman very much at peace with herself. Her aura also had a black thread woven through it. Grieving, obviously. This was, after all, the one-year anniversary of her brother's drowning. She said, "The home has been in my family for generations. We've all been coming out to Skull Island for over seventy-five years."

"Why is it called Skull Island?" asked Allison.

Edwin leaned forward again. "There's a Native American burial ground on the other side of the island. It's supposedly cursed."

"Skull Island and curses," said Allison, elbowing him. "Where's Scooby-Doo and Shaggy, too?"

Which had been, of course, my exact thought.

"Well, the curses are just legends," said Calvin Thurman, or Cal, one of the uncles. He was, I suspected, dying of a cancer. I knew this because of the dark spot of his kidney, a dark spot that was, literally, like a black hole, sucking in the color of his surrounding aura. Indeed, he leaned away from it, taking pressure off it.

He doesn't even know, I thought.

He held my gaze closely, and something seemed to pass between us. His eyes, I was certain, were trying to communicate something to me. He said, "Although there have been a few cases of unfortunate deaths."

"We don't talk about those," snapped Junior. "Not to strangers."

"Nonsense," said Cal, apparently not intimidated at all by his nephew, president of the company or not. He looked again at me. "It's in all the papers. Anyone can find that."

He continued looking at me. I looked at him. His eyes, I was certain, were pleading with me.

"Tell me about the deaths," I said uncomfortably. I had, of course, come across three such deaths in my own research of Skull Island. Were there some that I had missed?

But Junior's glowering stare finally cowered old Cal. He sighed deeply and winked at me. "Catch me later after I've had a few of these"—and he held up his Scotch—"and I'll tell you all."

He laughed. I laughed. No one else laughed.

Instead, Junior Thurman announced that tomorrow we would hold a memorial for his late father, George Thurman, whose death I had, unknown to the family, been hired to investigate. Junior went on: His late father had passed at this time last year, and he wanted to have a ceremony at the chapel located in the mausoleum.

Next, the conversation quickly turned to business. Tara turned and talked to me about my kids. All the while, I was aware of glances from various family members. Of course, some weren't glancing. Some were openly staring. Like Edwin Thurman. Edwin with his perpetual grin. Patricia, not so much.

Outside, the trees continued to sway and bend and appeared ready to snap, all while a sheet of rain swept over the grounds.

Welcome to Skull Island.

16.

We were back at the bungalow.

Just two college chums and their annoying new friend, all supposedly catching up—and most definitely not talking about murder.

Supposedly.

"You think they bought it?" asked Allison.

"Hard to say," said Tara. She'd brought a bottle of wine with her, of which we were all partaking. Some of us more vigorously than others.

"I think they bought it," said Allison, pouring herself yet another glass of wine.

"Tell me more about Edwin," I said to Tara.

"He's Junior's only son."

"Your cousin," I said.

"Right." Outside, rain slapped against the

bungalow's windows. Tree branches groaned overhead, as the bungalows were closer to the surrounding forest. "He was never much interested in the family's business."

"But I bet he's interested in the family money," said Allison, laughing. "Oops, sorry. Was that inappropriate?"

"No," said Tara. "Of course not. You guys are here to find answers to my grandfather's death. I'm not sure, at this point, if anything could be inappropriate, or if I would even care. And to answer your question...I'm not so sure about his desire for money."

"What do you mean?" I asked.

"He lives fairly simply. In fact, he often lives here."

"Living here isn't living simply," said Allison.

"True, but even while he's here, he lives simply. In fact, he prefers sleeping in the basement. On a cot, of all things."

"He's here a lot?" I asked.

"Often. In fact, he's rarely not here."

"What does he do here?"

"Nothing, as far as anyone knows."

"How did he take your grandfather's death?" I asked.

"That's the strange part," said Tara, looking up from her glass. "He didn't seem to take it hard at all."

"What do you mean?" I asked.

"I mean just that. He didn't appear overly

distraught."

"No tears?" asked Allison, piping in.

"None that I saw."

"Is there a room in the basement?" I asked.

"Of course, but it's so cold down there. Drafty. Miserable."

"Well, maybe he just wants to stay out of the way," said Allison. "You know, since he's here all the time."

"Maybe," said Tara.

Or maybe the cold doesn't bother him, I thought, sending it over to Allison.

A vampire? she thought back.

Yes. I thought. *I think. I can see his aura, so that's a problem.*

Problem, why?

I can't see vampires' auras.

Gotcha. So, is that why you had me shield my thoughts back at dinner?

I nodded and turned my attention back to Tara. "Were you here on the night of your grandfather's death?"

"Yes," she said. "We all were."

Tara next asked Allison for some more wine, who was only too willing to comply, and shortly, my friend and witness were both gone for the night.

I sighed, and made notes in my case file, all while the girls giggled and talked and got drunker and drunker. I made a mental note to fire Allison.

Rhetorically, of course.

17.

It was late.

Both Allison and Tara had drunk themselves into oblivion. Me, not so much. Other than a mild upset stomach, my two glasses of wine had had no effect.

I wasn't hungry yet, either. Two nights ago, I had drunk deeply from Allison's punctured wrist, as she'd looked away, winced, shuddered and broken out into a sweat. The wound had healed instantly, and by the time I had finished, she was no longer sweating. She had been grinning ghoulishly to herself. The act of me drinking from her gave her some sort of high.

Two sick puppies, I thought, as I pulled on a light jacket and flipped up the hood. My tennis shoes were already on, along with my jeans. I stood at the open door. The rain and wind had let up a little.

It also gave her more than a high, I knew. It sharpened her psychic abilities, of which she was already quite proficient. The act of me drinking from her had now made her into a sort of super psychic.

It was in much the same way that my own daughter's telepathic powers had increased due to her connection and proximity to me. And, for that matter, perhaps anyone connected to me.

I exited the bungalow, and hung a left toward the big house. It was 3:00 a.m., and I was alone in the night.

I couldn't have been happier.

Today had been a bit overwhelming to me. Too many people, too many introductions, too many handshakes, too many times I had apologized for my cold hands, too many times I had pretended to be normal.

I continued along the stone path, through the manicured gardens, past the epic barbeque and headed toward the pool. I paused at the surrounding gate and took in the scene around me. Trees lined the far edge of the massive estate. The bungalows dotted the perimeter of the grass, near the trees. The massive edifice of the Thurman home rose high into the night sky, like something medieval and ominous. The pool fence itself was only about six feet high. Tall enough to keep the kids out. I unlatched the gate.

The pool itself wasn't overtly big, perhaps slightly bigger than the standard pools. In the winter, I suspected the pool was covered. It wasn't winter. It was the beginning of summer, so all the pool toys were near: floating inner tubes, floating killer whales, floating rubber deck chair. The water rippled with the light rain and wind.

How could a grown man drown in his own pool?

I studied the area, noting the layout. There was a balcony directly above the pool. A part of me had suspected that George Thurman might have accidentally fallen into the pool—or been pushed. The balcony suggested that the possibility was still there.

The autopsy had been thorough. No drugs or alcohol, no blunt force. Skin clear, no lesions or scrapes or bruises. Blood tests came back negative, too. No poisoning. No sign of foul play.

Just a dead man in the water.

As I slowly circled the oval-shaped pool, my inner alarm began ringing a little louder. The sound was followed by footsteps, and then the appearance of a man.

A smiling man.

18.

It was Edwin, of course.

"Good evening, Samantha," he said.

He came closer and I saw that his hands were covered in dirt. Dirt was also under his fingernails. And it wasn't just dirt, but something else. Clay?

"Pardon my appearance. I was on an emergency dig."

"Digging what?" I asked, and was all too aware that my inner alarm was ringing even louder.

He came closer, grinning macabrely. He looked, quite frankly, insane. "Tell you what, Samantha. I will show you someday. How does that sound?"

"Weird as hell," I said.

He laughed. "Yes, I suppose it does sound sort of odd."

His aura, like that of Tara and old Cal, rippled with a dark thread-like energy. Except in Edwin, the darkness was more evident. I had assumed the darkness was a result of grief...now, I wasn't sure what to think.

"Why do you keep smiling like that?" I asked.

"Oh, I'm just a happy-go-lucky kind of guy. Made even happier now that you're here."

My inner alarm blared loudly. "What the hell does that mean?"

"Oh, nothing. We just so rarely get visitors here on our little island."

"I'm beginning to see why," I said, and found myself inching away from him.

He laughed. "Yes, we are an odd lot. Not exactly your typical family. And like most families, we have our hidden demons."

His words hit home. "You're one of them."

The young man continued grinning bizarrely. "One of whom, Samantha Moon?" He used my full name.

"You're a Dark Master," I said, using the term for the thing that lived in me, the thing that had mastered immortality, the thing that lived on through me using the darkest of magicks.

"Dark Master? I like that. I'm very flattered, Sam."

He flashed me another crazy smile, and now I saw something else within him. Something human. It was in his eyes, and it made a brief appearance. I saw the young man. The *real* Edwin Thurman.

Hidden. Pushed aside. Suffocated. But as quickly as he appeared, he disappeared again, like flotsam rising briefly to the ocean surface, only to be sucked under the dark waters again.

Edwin—or whoever was before me—stepped around me, clasping his hands behind his back. I got a very powerful psychic hit, and one that I knew was true.

"You're not like the others," I said.

He glanced at me, arching an eyebrow. "Oh? Do tell?"

"You are, if I'm correct, *permanently* present. You're not hidden in the background, not like the others, not like the thing within me."

"Not a thing, Sam." His annoyance surprised me. He paused, held my gaze, and added, "My sister."

I gasped and backed away some more.

"And I'm not saying that metaphorically, Samantha Moon. Residing within you is my sister, and someday soon—very, very soon—she and I will be together again."

19.

A low fog hung over the dark ocean.

The particles of light that only I could see seemed to disappear into the fog, to be absorbed by the mist. I might have gained a lot of gifts since becoming the thing that I am, but one of them, apparently, was not the ability to see into fog.

I was sitting at the edge of a small cliff. Waves crashed thirty feet or so below. Some of the spray reached me, sprinkling my skin and lips. I didn't lick my lips. Even salt spray would upset my stomach.

The path from the house was a well-maintained one, as I suspected this cliff side retreat was a favorite hangout for the family. During the daytime, I was sure one could see for miles and miles. Now, not so much, even to my eyes.

To say that the conversation with Edwin had shaken me was an understatement.

His sister?

Obviously, not a Thurman sister, for I hadn't been talking to the real Edwin Thurman. No, I had been talking to something ancient and evil. Another dark master who sought entry back into our world.

And not just any dark master, I suspected.

No, he didn't have to hide in the shadows of the living, like that which had entered Kingsley and me...and now Fang. No, whoever he was, he had taken over the real Edwin Thurman—completely and totally.

Who he was, I didn't know. But he was powerful.

Perhaps even the most powerful of all.

And his sister was in me.

Jesus.

I suddenly wished I wasn't sitting on the cliff's edge, in the cold and rain and wind, but sleeping with my kids, one on either side of me, their warm bodies giving me warmth in return. I could almost smell Tammy's hair. I could almost even smell Anthony's stinky feet.

As the wind and rain picked up, drenching me to the bone, I did the only thing this middle-aged divorcée mother of two could do:

I took off my clothes.

And stepped to the edge of the cliff.

I summoned the single flame in my thoughts.

Held it.

Saw the image of the beast.

The beast I would become.

And then I leaped out as far and wide as I could, arching up and over the pounding surf.

The transformation was instant, taking hold of me before I plunged into the rocks below.

I was soon flying. High above the island. High above the fog. High above, even, the snoring Allison.

It was up here where I found my sanctuary, my peace, my escape. I was all too aware that it was the thing that lived within me that gave me this very ability. The thing I could never escape.

We'll see, I thought, and began flapping my wings.

20.

Allison and I were sitting together at breakfast.

I'd managed about three hours of sleep before Allison literally woke me from the dead. Now, we sat with the other Thurmans—or a few of them at least—on a wide balcony that overlooked the grounds. As Allison ate and I drank water, I caught her up to speed on the night's events. When I was finished, I said, "Your mouth's hanging open."

"It tends to do that when I'm shocked shitless."

I shushed her. Although we were alone at our little patio table, there were still other Thurmans eating nearby. The morning had been shockingly clear and warm, so much so that breakfast had been served outside. There was a nearby table filled with heaps of eggs and breakfast meats and pancakes.

Someone had cooked up a storm. Many nodded at us as we sat and talked. Noticeably absent was Edwin Thurman and our hostess, Tara.

"And where is the man of the hour?" asked Allison. She was, of course, talking about Edwin.

"In his room," I said.

"You mean, the basement?"

"Right," I said.

"And you know this how?"

"I've got mad skills," I said. Although Allison was a close friend, she was still a new friend. She didn't know the extent of what I could do. Truth was, I didn't know the extent of what I could do either. So, for an explanation, I gave her a glimpse now into my memory, showing her what I'd done—and what I had seen.

She blinked after a moment. "You can remote sense?"

"I guess so, yes."

"Geez, the government's been training psychics for decades trying to get them to do what you can do."

"Well, I can't see very far, maybe only a few hundred feet or so."

"Far enough. I saw the image of him lying there on his little cot, sleeping. Very clear image. Very precise."

"Very weird," I said.

"Well, weird or not, it's helpful...and why the hell is he lying on a cot, in the basement, in this beautiful home?"

"Maybe they ran out of beds," I said.

"Or maybe it's because he's a vampire."

I shook my head and lowered my voice. "No. Not a vampire. He's something else. He's different."

"Different, how?"

"Greater. More powerful."

She caught the meaning of my words and also caught my own vaguely formulated thought. "Sam," she said. "Do you really think he might be the greatest of them all?"

Allison and I had previously discussed the thing that resides in me. She understood that it was this thing that fueled me and gave me eternal life. She understood that this thing needed to be fed, and blood was its choice. She understood that the powers within it emanated out to me, making me stronger and stronger.

I said, "I don't know yet. I don't know much about these entities. I don't know why they've been banished, and why they want back in. I don't understand the kind of magicks needed to give them access to me, and to live within me forever."

"But you think the thing that lives in Edwin Thurman might be the strongest of them all."

"That's what my gut is telling me."

She snorted. "Well, I can tell you one thing: I can tell you who's high on my suspect list of who killed George Thurman."

"We don't know if he killed him," I said.

"Well, he certainly sounds like he's got it in for

you, Sam. Did he really say his sister is inside you?"

"Yes."

"God, you vampires are weird."

"Thanks."

"So, what's the game plan, Sammie? Other than me keeping you alive."

"You keeping me alive?"

"Someone's got to, kiddo. My sensitivities may not be as strong as yours, but I am getting a very, very strong feeling that not all is as it seems on Skull Island."

"Very melodramatic," I said.

"And very real."

My cell phone went off. I looked down at it: Danny. The ex. Allison saw it, too.

"You going to answer?" she asked.

"No."

It rang again. I drummed my fingers.

"Fine," I said irritably, and clicked on.

21.

"Sam, I want to see the kids more often."

"Why?"

"Because I love them."

"Why?"

"Because they're my kids, goddamn it."

"Sorry, but I'm going to need more than that."

"Sam, I'm warning you."

"Or what?"

"Jesus, Sam. All I'm asking is for you to let me see my kids—our kids—a little more. I only see them, what, every other week for a few hours. Supervised."

"You also happen to own a sleazy strip club and date even sleazier strippers."

"Hey," said Allison, looking up from her smart

phone. "I used to be a stripper."

I covered the mouthpiece and lowered my voice. "Were you sleazy?"

"Sleazy, no. Good, yes."

I rolled my eyes and uncovered the phone. "So, you see my point, then," I said to Danny.

"I see that you're a controlling bitch."

"As always, nice talking to you, Danny."

"Wait, wait!" he screeched as I made a move to hang up. "Don't hang up. I'm sorry."

I didn't hang up, but I didn't say anything either. I looked out across the outdoor deck. So beautiful. This could have been a resort.

"You there, Sam?"

"I'm here."

"Sorry, I didn't mean that."

"Yes, you did."

"Okay, I did, but it's only because you're being a little unreasonable."

"Danny, I'm going to say this with all the sincerity I can. I really don't give a shit what you think about me, but I do know one thing, and one thing only: until you sell that sleazebag of a strip club you own and quit bringing your skank-whores home, you will never, ever be alone with my kids."

Someone from a nearby table looked over at me. Oops. I might have raised my voice a little.

"You can't tell me when I can or cannot see my kids."

"I can and I did."

"I'm giving up the law firm, Sam."

I snorted. "To run the strip club full time?"

"It's a lot of money, Sam. Easy money."

"You are choosing easy money over your kids. Strippers over your kids."

"You have it wrong, Sam. I don't date the girls."

Just hearing the word "girls" made my skin crawl. "No," I said, "you just fuck them."

"You can't tell me what to do, Sam. Who to see and who not to see. How to live my life. How to make money."

"No, but I can tell you this."

He sighed. "What?"

"You will never, ever be alone with my kids."

And I clicked off the phone.

Emphatically.

22.

"You've got that look in your eye," said Allison.
"What look?"

"That don't-mess-with-me-or-I'm-gonna-rip-out
-your-throat look." As she spoke, she slowly
reached over and gently pried my fingers from my
iPhone. The bottom corner of the phone's screen
was already cracked from my last conversation with
Danny.

"Remember," she said. "He's a total pig."

"And that," I said, getting up, "is why I keep
you around."

"You keep me around?" said Allison, grabbing
her plate of unfinished eggs and hurrying after me.
"Maybe it's the other way around. Maybe I keep

you around."

"Sure," I said, and picked up my pace.

"Hey, where are we going?"

I opened the French door that led from the balcony into the magnificent kitchen. I looked back at her. "We're looking for a killer, remember?"

"Well, I think we found him."

"Maybe," I said. "Maybe not."

"So, where are we going?"

"I've got some investigator stuff to do."

"And what am I supposed to do?"

I motioned to the others who were still sitting outside on the deck, enjoying what was, I suspected, rare sunshine. Indeed, storm clouds were already gathering on the far horizon. And if I wasn't mistaken, they looked even nastier than the ones from yesterday.

"Do what you do best," I said. "Talk."

"Gee, thanks."

"Mingle. Get me the lowdown. Let me know who sets off your own inner alarm system."

She opened her mouth to say something else, but I shooed her back outside. She pouted a moment or two, then stuck out her tongue and headed back out onto the deck.

I paused in the kitchen, closed my eyes, and mentally searched the home again. I saw everyone, even Edwin asleep on his cot in the basement. One person was still noticeably absent: Tara. Perhaps she was out of my range.

So, I zeroed in on the one person I was looking

for, and headed off.

Deeper into the massive home.

23.

I soon got lost.

I backtracked down a hallway or two, rounded a corner, passed an actual conservatory with its domed, glass ceiling, and found myself in the library.

No, I didn't see Professor Plum or Colonel Mustard. Definitely, I didn't see a candlestick, whatever that was. I did see, however, an older gentleman reading a book and drinking from a highball glass. The amber liquid in the glass wasn't, I suspected, lemonade.

Cal Thurman, George Thurman's brother, looked up from the latest James Patterson novel, this one called *Death, Sweet Death*, and smiled broadly when he saw me.

"Allison, right?"

"Close," I said. "Allison's my friend. I'm Samantha."

He chuckled. "Hey, at my age, anything close is a good sign. The other day I called my wife Rick."

"Who's Rick?"

"No clue. Have a seat."

I grinned and sat in the chair next to him. He asked if I wanted a drink, indicating a bar nearby. I mentioned that this was the first library I'd seen with a full service bar. He laughed and said he would drink to that, and did. Then he poured himself another and sat back down next to me. I noted the time: 11:45. Not even noon.

"So, what can I do you for?" he asked, and, with one gulp, nearly finished his fresh glass of the hard stuff.

"You suggested that I see you about some, ah, strange occurrences that have been happening on the island. I'm interested in hearing more about the curse."

"Did I?"

"Yes."

"Was I drunk?"

"You were drinking, yes."

He laughed. "That might explain it. Sure, yes. There's rumors this island is cursed. Dates all the way back to when, hell, I don't know, probably back to the Native Americans. Even before the white man came, the Native Americans were at war over this island. From what we gather, there was a lot of bloodshed here. Not to mention a shipwreck or two."

I'd read about the island having some history, and that it had been the location of a few tribal skirmishes, but I wasn't aware of a lot of bloodshed. I asked him to explain further.

"We've found two burial sites on the north side of the island. We're on the south side. And not just burial sites, but battle sites, too. Skulls cleaved nearly in half, severed arms and legs, and gashes to necks and ribs. Dozens and dozens of such bodies."

"Found where?" I asked.

"Mostly in the ground, but some were in a tunnel system that appears to run underneath the island. Edwin has taken an interest in the tunnels, and so has Tara, for that matter."

He eyed me earnestly. Granted, his eyes were bloodshot, but he was imploring me, I think, to read deeper into his words.

He continued, "Back in the day, my father was going to build on the north end, along the peninsula, where he would have panoramic views of the Sound and the city of Victoria. Instead, he built here, in the woods, which was really the only other viable spot."

"What made him change course?"

"The hauntings. The workers getting spooked. And, of course, the deaths. Which, of course, leads us back to the curse."

He explained further. "Two workers had been killed at the old site, both having fallen from ladders. Both deaths had been unexplained, as they had been alone. Another worker had heard one of the men scream. Sounded like he'd seen a ghost...and then plummeted to his death."

"Perhaps, he screamed on the way down," I suggested.

Cal shook his blocky head. "No. It was described as the most blood-curdling scream anyone had ever heard, followed by another scream. Which, I assume, was the poor bastard falling. Anyway, that's when the talk of curses began."

"So, what happened next?"

"My father decided to change course. And build the home on the south side, where we're at now."

"And no more instances of curses?"

"Samantha, there are always instances of curses."

"What do you mean?"

He opened his mouth, and suddenly shut it again. Tight. The smallest grin curled his lips. The same creepy grin I had seen on the faces of Edwin and Tara.

"I...I'm afraid I can't talk about the curse anymore, Samantha."

Cal seemed to be struggling with something, fighting something. My inner alarm began chiming softly. What the hell was going on?

I decided to change course. "Was your brother's death associated with the curse?"

"I..." he began and closed his mouth again. He was shaking now. And sweating. A reaction to being drunk? I didn't know.

I waited, silent, listening to my inner alarm growing steadily louder. Now I could see the same black ribbons circulating through his aura. The same ribbons I had seen in others. Ribbons I had rarely, if ever, seen before.

"What happened to your brother?" I pushed.

"I...can't...speak about it."

His voice sounded strangled, as if his throat had suddenly been restricted.

"Mr. Thurman, are you okay?"

He looked at me with pleading eyes. Then he gasped once, twice, and seemed to find his breath. "I'm...never okay, my dear."

"I don't understand—"

"The curse," he gasped, and his voice seemed to restrict again.

The ribbons of ethereal darkness swelled a little more, looking more like black snakes now, weaving through his aura, in and out, in and out.

"What about the curse, Mr. Thurman?"

He began shaking. He reminded me of my son when he was fighting off his sickness. Cal Thurman was fighting something. What it was, I didn't know.

He suddenly opened his eyes wide, gasping. "It has us all, Samantha. It controls us all. We are not free. We are never free. Please help, please—"

The black snake that had been circulating through his aura, rose up suddenly. I saw its dark, diamond-shaped head moving rapidly through the man. It rose higher and higher—and plunged into his throat.

Cal gasped and grabbed his neck.

Now the snake coiled around and around his throat like a boa constrictor, squeezing tighter and tighter. Cal gasped and lurched to the side, screaming. In a blink of an eye, his aura went from pale blue, to deep black, and as I screamed for help, Cal Thurman looked at me with pleading eyes, and then quit breathing.

Forever.

24.

I immediately performed CPR.

All while I called out for help. Someone nearby heard me. A girl. I told her to get help. She stared at me for a moment, then took off running, her feet pounding along the polished tiles.

I went back to my CPR, doing all I could to get Cal's heart beating, to get him breathing again, and by the time the first adults arrived—Junior and his wife, followed shortly by Tara and Allison—I was certain that Cal was quite dead.

***

Jesus, Sam, what happened? asked Allison.

We were all sitting in the great room. All

seventeen of us. Cal was still in the library, lying under a sheet. Further attempts to resuscitate him had gone for naught.

Are your thoughts protected? I asked.

Yes, of course.

Something killed him. I watched it kill him. I'm seriously freaked out.

Allison snapped her head around and stared at me. She wasn't the only one who stared at me. Most people in the room were looking at me. Also in the room was Tara. I'd been too busy and shaken to notice when she'd returned. Edwin hadn't stopped looking my direction. The sky beyond the big windows was a nasty gray. The first of the day's raindrops had begun to splatter against the glass. Jagged bolts of lightning occasionally lit up the underbelly of the heavy clouds. Junior, who had been on his cell phone in the hallway, came into the room.

"The Island County Sheriff can't make it out today," he reported. He looked ten years older than when I'd last seen him. He had, after all, just lost his uncle. "Nor can the paramedics, nor anyone else, for that matter."

"Why?" asked a little girl. She was, I knew, one of Junior's granddaughters.

"Because of the storm, honey."

I was holding my phone. I wanted to text Fang. To text Kingsley even. I didn't feel comfortable texting Russell yet. The poor guy was just beginning to know me. I couldn't lay something like this on him. What was I supposed to say? That I'd seen some dark entity strangle a man? For a new relationship, that might be a deal breaker.

Fang would have understood, and so would've Kingsley. Hell, so would have Detective Sherbet. For now, I was left with only Allison.

Gee thanks, Sam.

Oops, I thought. *You know what I mean. The others are, you know...*

Freaky like you?

Right.

Outside, the wind had clearly picked up. The tall evergreens were once again swaying and bending. Rain splattered harder, driven into the window. A lawn chair outside scuttled over the grounds, rolling like a tumbleweed.

Did you really watch him die, Sam?

Yes, and I'm still shaking.

I gave her a glimpse of my own memory of the event, reliving the moment the darkness appeared from his aura and reached up to his throat. I relived his last few words, too:

"It has us all, Samantha. It controls us all. We are not free. We are never free..."

Jesus, came Allison's reply. *Was he poisoned?*

Maybe, I thought. But I suspected it was something else, something that I didn't entirely understand, but it had to do with his last words to me: *It controls us all.*

Allison, who'd been following my train of thought as best she could, formulated the words that

I had been searching for: *Sam, you think that, on some level, that whatever has control over Edwin, also had control over Cal?*

But not just the two of them, I thought grimly.

All of them? asked Allison.

Maybe.

Junior turned his attention to me. "Samantha, I can't express to you how thankful I am for your efforts on behalf of my uncle. I'm sure that you did all you could to save his life."

"I'm sorry I couldn't do more," I said.

"What, exactly, *did* you do?" asked Patricia, Junior's wife.

Her aura, I noted, was not rippled with the same black ribbon I had seen in some of the others. Her aura was a biting green. I opened my mouth to speak, but instead, looked around me. Junior, I noted, had a black ribbon woven through his aura. I looked again at Edwin: the same black ribbon. I looked at the kids. They all had black ribbons, some thicker than others. All of them. I'd never seen this before. Not like this, and not in the same pattern, and not with so many people.

What the hell was going on? I wondered.

"Standard CPR," I said, finally.

"Where did you learn this standard CPR?"

I glanced over at Tara. She was holding her breath. I glanced over at Edwin. He was grinning knowingly. The jig, I was quite certain, was up.

I said, "At the FBI Academy."

"Are you a federal agent, Samantha?"

"Not anymore."

Junior, who had been standing, stepped threateningly before me, arms crossed. "Then what the hell are you, Samantha?"

I looked over at Tara, who was standing near the arched opening into the great room. Her aura, I noted, was still rippled with the same black ribbon.

"I'm a private investigator," I said. "And my name's Samantha Moon."

25.

"What's going on, dear?" asked Patricia.

She got up and stood next to her husband. He slipped an arm around her waist and studied me, the picture of a loving couple. I noted that she didn't have black ribbons coiling through her otherwise bright green aura. Green, the color of envy or distrust. In this situation, I didn't blame her.

"I'm not sure, honey," he said, and I believed him. I felt his confusion and hers, too.

I noted that the black ribbons that wound through his aura had picked up slightly. I looked over at Edwin. His ribbons were thicker, like mountaineering ropes, twisting through his aura.

Junior turned his attention to his niece, Tara. "I want to know what's going on, young lady, and I want to know now. Why did you bring a private investigator to the island?"

"And her assistant," Allison piped up.

Except no one was listening. All eyes turned to Tara, and as they did so, I noted something very, very curious. Her own black ribbons, which had been no thicker than a half inch, suddenly swelled —doubling, tripling their size. Now they veritably pulsated, swirling faster and faster around her.

Curiouser and curiouser.

I looked over at Edwin to compare his own dark aura...and was equally stunned to see that his once-thick ribbons had now shrunk to thinner ribbons...in fact, only small traces of black showed in him. He was shaking his head and blinking hard, as if coming out of a deep sleep.

All this happened while Tara Thurman stared at me. No, leered at me. Menacingly.

What the hell? I thought.

Edwin continued rubbing his face and appeared by all indications, to be waking.

What the double hell?

What's wrong, Sam? thought Allison, picking up on my thoughts. She and I still had our ultra-secret line of communication open. *What's going on?*

I'll explain later, I thought. *If I can.*

Tara leaned forward on the elegant, camel-back sofa. She crossed her legs slowly and wiped some lint off her knee. As she did so, one thing was certain...that damned creepy smile...the same one that seemed to be a permanent fixture on Edwin's face, was now obvious on her face. I'd seen it on her, too.

The same smile, I thought. *It's body-hopping.*

Body-what, Sam? What's going on?

Not now, I thought.

Tara continued wiping away at the speck. As she did so, she shuddered slightly, and I suspected I knew what was going on. It was getting used to her body.

"Tara?" prodded Junior impatiently. "What the devil is going on here?"

Good choice of words, I thought.

After a moment, with the same too-big smile plastered to her otherwise pretty face, Tara finally looked up at him, then over at me.

"Yes, I hired Samantha Moon, private investigator extraordinaire," said Tara. Except she didn't sound like Tara. Not really; at least not to my ears. The black ribbons that wound through her aura were thicker than ever, and pulsated like something radioactive.

"But why?" asked Junior. He didn't seem to notice the change in his niece. Nor did anyone else. No, not true. On second thought, Patricia was biting her lower lip and looking from Edwin—who was still blinking hard—to Tara, who was smiling psychotically.

She knows, I thought.

Knows what? asked Allison.

Later!

"I hired her to investigate Grandpa George's death," said Tara.

"But why? Why would you do that?"

Tara was looking at me, but it wasn't Tara. It was the thing that had been in Edwin—and was now in her. "I wasn't thinking straight, uncle. I was...I was confused. I thought maybe a private investigator could help us...perhaps shed light on what happened."

Junior crossed the room and sat next to his brother's daughter. "Grandpa George drowned, Tari."

"I know...but *why* did he drown?"

Junior gazed at her, then turned and looked at his wife. She shrugged. He sighed. I sensed no deception coming from them. I sensed no concealing of truth. They were legitimately at a loss for answers.

Finally, Junior said, "We don't know why he drowned, honey, but the medical report assured us there was no foul play."

Tara nodded, although the plastered smile remained on her face. She reminded me of the Joker from Batman. She started nodding, and now tears appeared on her high cheekbones. Tears and that big, disturbing smile.

"I just wanted help. I just wanted answers." She pointed at me. "And she was so willing to help, so willing to—no, I shouldn't say it."

"So willing to take your money?" finished Junior.

Tara looked at him, then at me, and nodded. Allison gasped next to me and made to stand up. I held her back. Junior turned and looked at me. "When the storm clears, you're on the next boat out of here."

"I don't think so," I said.

Something dark clouded over him. No, this wasn't a body-jumping dark entity. It was his own self-righteous anger. "You will leave, Samantha Moon, even if I have to make you."

"With all due respect, Mr. Thurman," I said. "I was hired to do a job, and I intend to finish it."

Someone in the room inhaled sharply. Tara, peeking out from behind her uncle, smiled even broader. Junior strode over and stood before me, threateningly. I didn't get threatened by angry men, even back before my immortal days. I was still sitting on the loveseat next to Allison—even though, I was fairly certain, we weren't in love. Junior stood over six feet tall and was used to getting his way. His uncle, Cal, was lying dead just down the hallway. This wasn't a time for him to make a scene or to make things even worse than they were.

I telepathically reached out to him. This was something I'd recently discovered I could do, something that, apparently, most vampires could do. For me, it was still new—and still something I wasn't comfortable doing.

Calm, I thought. *All is okay. I'm just here to help. I'm not the enemy.*

Junior blinked, and then unclenched his fists. He swayed slightly, looked at me confusedly, then turned and went back to his wife. He took her hand and she looked at him, also confused.

I stood, and so did Allison.

"I'm sorry for your loss," I said to the room in general. "Cal seemed like a good man. But I've also been hired to do a job—a job I intend to finish, one way or another. Each of you can expect a visit from me." I looked at Patricia Thurman, Junior's wife. "And I'll be seeing you first."

She blinked with the telepathic suggestion I'd also given her, and with that, Allison and I left the room.

26.

We were back at the bungalow.

Allison had poured us two glasses of wine and now, once we had dried off and were in some warm clothing, we sat around the small dinette table that also afforded a view of both the back yard and the brick mansion beyond. Rain slanted nearly sideways across the window, like so many silver daggers. We both kept our eyes mostly on the big house.

Allison was wearing a sweater and jeans and the thickest socks I'd ever seen. "What did you see, Sam?" she asked me.

Good question. I'd been asking myself the same thing since we'd left the house and dashed through the rain like two schoolgirls at recess.

"How good are you at seeing auras?" I asked her.

"Pretty good, but not as good as you. You see details that I can't—heck, that I don't think even the best psychics can see. You know, you could make a lot of money as a psychic, Sammie. Just saying."

"I'll pass. So you didn't see anything unusual about any of the Thurmans' auras?"

"Nothing that stood out, why?"

So, I told her about the shadowy ribbons, or ropes, that wove through all the Thurmans' auras like so many lassos.

"Through all of them?"

"All," I said, and she must have caught my next thought.

"You mean all the *blood* relatives," she said.

"Exactly." I gave her a glimpse of my own memory, so that she could see the shadows for herself.

"What is it?" she said after a moment, her mouth hanging open.

"I don't honestly know."

"The black ropes appear to be...binding them," said Allison.

"Good point," I said.

"Like it's holding them hostage."

I shuddered. Outside, a magnificent bolt of lightning appeared, rending the gray sky in two. The bolt could have come straight from Asgard, hurled from the mighty Thor himself. Or, if I was lucky, from Chris Hemsworth. The bolt was followed immediately by a clap of thunder so loud that Allison jumped.

After a moment, she said, "What the hell is going on, Sam?"

"I don't know, kiddo. But there's more."

Next, I told her about the change I'd seen in Tara, and, subsequently, the change I'd seen in Edwin. And not just changes of the physical kind, but within their auras. I showed her mental images as I spoke.

Allison nodded along, even as she was looking a little pale. When I was finished, she said, "Yeah, I thought our hostess was looking a little odd. All that freaky smiling. Thought maybe she'd hit the mimosas a little early."

"I don't think so," I said. "There's something else going on here."

"What? I'll admit, I'm lost."

I drummed my fingers on the table and watched as the back door to the big house opened and a woman emerged, a woman I wasn't surprised to see at all. She popped open an umbrella—which was promptly blown free from her hands, to tumble endlessly across the backyard. She seemed confused at first, then threw on her hood, and dashed across the big back yard.

"I think," I said, watching the sprinting figure, "that the entity is body-hopping."

"Body-hopping?"

"Or body-jumping, or whatever it's called."

"Do you have any idea how crazy that sounds,

Sam?"

"No more crazy than everything else."

"Good point. And this entity isn't just any entity, is it?" she asked me.

"No," I said. "It might just be the strongest of them all."

"And you know that how?"

"Call it a hunch," I said. "And there's something else?"

"What?"

I nodded toward the window. "We have company."

27.

We moved to the bungalow's living room.

"These places aren't bugged, are they?" asked Allison.

"No," said Patricia Thurman, looking wet and miserable, and nothing like the socialite I knew she was. Her canvas shoes were soaked through and muddy. The hems of her white pants were muddy as well. Her jacket had kept most of the water off, but her face was still dripping wet. She dabbed it with a bath towel that Allison had given her.

"I don't know why I'm here," she said.

I knew why she was here, but didn't say anything. As I'd left the family, of course, I had given her a very strong telepathic suggestion to come see me.

You devil, thought Allison.

Our secret, I thought, and turned to Patricia. "Maybe you're here because there's something you want to tell us."

"You know, get off your chest," piped in Allison.

Patricia Thurman, who was probably forty-eight years old, but looked, after all her plastic surgery, forty-six years old, also appeared flummoxed. She really didn't know why she had decided to come out into the rain to speak with me. But now that she was here, I could see she was warming up to the idea.

"Well, I'm not in the habit of discussing my family to strangers, you see."

"I understand," I said. "Your niece hired me to help. She felt she had a good reason to."

"And, with Cal dying, maybe she does," said Mrs. Thurman. She tried on a weak smile for size, but it didn't last. It faltered and her lower lip quivered. "God, not Cal, too. Honestly, that's still sinking in."

"You liked Cal?" I asked, just to get the conversation moving. Sometimes the simplest questions led to a windfall of answers. We would see, especially since I just encouraged her telepathically to open up to me a little more.

"Cal was always kind to me, always full of laughter. Always drunk."

I smiled. "There's a lot of drinking with the Thurmans."

"Not that there's any problem with that," added

Allison, which earned her a scowl from me.

"Aw, yes," said Patricia, ignoring Allison. "The drinking. The endless drinking. Well, maybe that's part of the curse, too. Had Cal told you about the curse?"

"He didn't have a chance," I said.

"I'm not surprised."

"What do you mean?"

"Never mind, I've said too much as it is."

She made a move to stand and I gently prodded her to relax, sending her a comforting thought that should have put her at ease: *You are among friends, it's warm in here, no one will hurt you, we're only trying to help.*

"Would you like some coffee, Mrs. Thurman?" I asked.

"Yes, please, that would be delightful." She smiled and blinked and then frowned a little, no doubt surprised to hear the words issue from her mouth.

"Allison?" I said.

"Yeah?" She'd been sitting at the edge of her seat.

"Could you make Mrs. Thurman some coffee?"

"Oh, yeah, right. I'm on it."

She got up and headed into the adjoining kitchen, working quickly, but listening, I knew, to the conversation going on in the living room.

"Tell me more about the curse, Mrs. Thurman."

"I don't want to."

"Why not?"

"Because the family isn't supposed to talk about it."

"What happens if someone talks about it?"

"They die."

"Because of the curse?"

"Because of...something," she said.

The smell of fresh coffee soon filled the small bungalow, awakening an old need in me, an old craving. I had once loved coffee more than life itself.

Mrs. Thurman was closed off to me again, and I prodded her further. But first, I wanted to make sure she was safe talking to me. Yes, I needed information, but, no, I didn't want to jeopardize her life in the process. After all, I had seen the dark snake rise up through Cal's solar plexus, to strangle the life from him...from the inside out.

Which, of course, left no mark.

Just like with George Thurman in the pool. Allison's thoughts appeared in my mind as she stepped out of the kitchen with two cups of steaming coffee. One for each of them...and none for me. I sighed.

I nodded. *Which could explain why there were no marks on George Thurman.*

And why the coroner could only conclude he'd drowned accidentally.

As Patricia Thurman accepted the coffee, looking a bit confused as to why she was still here, when, no doubt, her every instinct told her to leave, I gave her another gentle prodding, encouraging her further to tell me more of the family curse, but without divulging so much as to put herself at risk.

When she was done sipping her coffee, she smiled sweetly at me, crossed her legs, and said, "You were asking me about the family curse?"

"Yes," I said. "I was wondering if it's, well, real?"

She nodded and sipped more coffee and would have looked very elegant, if not for her muddy pants. "Oh, yes. It's very, very real."

"Does the curse extend to you?"

"No, not directly. Indirectly, maybe."

"What do you mean?"

"It means that if anyone in my family knows that I'm talking to you about the curse, I might not live to see tomorrow." She smiled at me again then added pleasantly: "And neither will either of you."

Allison put down her coffee. That was, apparently, enough for her to lose her desire for the good stuff.

"The curse is passed down through the blood," I said. "Which is why you're not directly affected by it."

"Why, that's very observant, Ms. Moon. I can see why Tara hired you. Yes, the curse has been passed down through the generations."

"Dating back to when?"

"Conner Thurman."

I knew the name. "George's and Cal's father."

"Yes, the bastard who caused this mess," she said and turned to Allison. "Do you have any sugar, dear?"

"Um, I dunno. Let me check."

While Allison went searching for the sugar, I asked Patricia to elaborate on Conner's involvement with the curse. Which she did.

And what a curse it was.

28.

"It all began ninety years ago," Patricia revealed.

"Conner Thurman was an ambitious business-man. Perhaps too ambitious. He'd always looked for an edge over his competition. He'd come upon a secretive club of elite world leaders, corporate leaders, politicians and celebrities. Not exactly the Masons or the Illuminati, per se, but certainly a group of rich and powerful people who enjoyed their elite status. They called themselves 'The Society'."

Admittedly, I was riveted to Patricia's unfolding tale.

"Conner Thurman wasn't quite in their elite status yet. Yes, he'd had some success in the hotel industry, but certainly nothing that would have given him a golden ticket into The Society. After all, few ever got the golden ticket.

"Conner was enamored by them. He wanted to rub elbows with them. And he did, sometimes. Just enough to whet his appetite further. The occasional golfing trip. The occasional dinner with some of the others. Always occasionally. Never was he fully immersed. Never was he truly one of them."

This was getting good. I nodded at her to go on.

"And, yes, he very much wanted to be one of them. Joining The Society meant that nothing would stop him or his business. He would crush his competition. He would gain the only competitive edge he would ever need: he would have The Society on his side.

"That's all he would need.

And so, he hung around. He accepted their meager offerings and not-so-secretly wished for more. He wished very hard for more."

"As we all do," I said.

"Be careful what you wish for," said Patricia, raising her empty cup, indicating that she wanted more coffee. I looked at Allison. Allison looked at me.

"Fine," said my friend grumpily. She snatched Mrs. Thurman's mug from her hand.

"Your assistant has a bit of an attitude," said Mrs. Thurman, and not too quietly.

A coffee cup banged. The coffee pot banged. The refrigerator slammed.

"Here, madam," said Allison a moment later—and a little bit too sweetly.

"Thank you, dear," said Mrs. Thurman, rolling her eyes.

"You were saying," I said, prodding her mentally. "Something about wishes..."

"Yes, Conner Thurman would get exactly what he wanted...and his family, even to this day—and perhaps forevermore—will continue to suffer because of it."

She went on. "Conner had been invited to a secret ritual. He had been told that it was an initiation ceremony. Conner was beside himself. Was he really, finally, truly going to be one of them? He hoped to God—and so he went with great expectations."

Initiation ceremony? Now it was starting to really sound like a creepy cult.

"And then?" I said expectantly.

"The ceremony was held outdoors at a private retreat. A gated, private retreat, complete with armed guards. It was the first time Conner had ever been to the Retreat. He would never divulge its location. But it was somewhere in upstate New York."

"Excuse me," said Allison, breaking in. "How do you know all this?"

"Because I'm one of them, dear. I may not be blood, no, but I am very much one of them."

She smiled sweetly and drank her coffee. Actually, not so sweetly. There was a darkness in her eyes. This woman, I suspected, had a cold-hearted streak in her.

She went on as I shuddered slightly.

"The ritual quickly got out of hand. There were dozens of men in various stages of dress. Naked prostitutes. An altar covered in blood. Fresh blood. Conner felt sick and turned to leave but was not permitted to. No, he had already seen too much. His choices were simple: become one of them, or join the fate of the others."

"He still wanted to be one of them?" I asked.

"Badly. After all, what were a few prostitutes?"

Sick, I thought.

Patricia Thurman continued, "One such prostitute was splayed out on the altar. Naked. Screaming. Begging for mercy. Conner was given a stone blade that he was told was imbued with supernatural power. He was told to use it to kill the screaming woman, to silence her, to sacrifice her."

I had a good idea what had happened from that point on. Patricia kept talking.

"He had looked at her only briefly, and then turned his face away as he drove the dagger deep into her chest while she shrieked and fought and finally died. His hands were soaked with her blood and he wanted to break down and weep. He wanted to plunge the dagger into his own heart, too. How could he do this to an innocent human being?"

Patricia was on a roll now. I don't think she could have shut up if she'd wanted to.

"Next, he was quickly pulled into a cabin, and

over to another kind of altar. He had passed their test, apparently. They were well-pleased with him. They had him shower and dress in fine robes.

"He didn't feel like showering. He didn't care that they were pleased with him. He wanted to turn himself in to the police. He wanted to run away forever. He wanted to drop to his knees and weep.

"But everything was happening so fast. So very fast. The shower, the robe, and now kneeling before the new altar.

"Others were there, too. Others who seemed pleased with him. Others who were hooded and robed just like him."

Allison looked at me with chagrin. Patricia kept going.

"He was told it was time to become one of them. He shook his head and said no, that he no longer wanted to become one of them. He was told it was too late. The process had begun.

"They spoke of untold wealth and power. They reminded him what a privilege it was to be one of them, The Society. Still, he continued to shake his head, weeping into his hood. Listening again to the woman who had begged for her life."

Why had he killed her? I wondered.

"But the longer he was with them, and the longer he knelt before the strange altar, the further away the woman's cries became. He was told that she was nothing. A whore. A test. To forget about her. To think of himself and his family. His legacy. His empire that was to come.

"Yes, he wanted an empire. They would create it for him. They would help build it for him. They would pave the way for him. No one would stop his empire. No one. Not even God."

Patricia had pulled the God card.

She went on, "He was nodding now. Yes, he desperately wanted it. After all, he had proven himself, right? He had done all they asked, right? Surely he deserved the keys to the kingdom.

"Yes, it was time. It was time for him to claim his destiny. For himself, his family and future generations.

"Not yet, they told him. There was still a final step. A final act of loyalty. A final price."

I was pretty sure I knew what it was.

***

Patricia paused in her retelling, looking haggard and drained, and far from the beauty queen she'd once been.

Years of a family curse will do that to you, came Allison's thoughts.

Patricia looked like she wouldn't go on—couldn't go on. I respected that. I knew this was hard on her, even with my gentle prodding.

So, I finished the tale for her, as I suspected I knew the ending. "He sold his soul," I said.

Patricia Thurman snapped her head around. Her mouth dropped open a little. The look of shock segued into grim defeat. She nodded. "Yes. And not just his soul. Everyone in the family's soul. Everyone. Every future generation." She paused, and seemed tempted to ask Allison for another cup of coffee, but set the mug on the table in front of her instead. She uncrossed her legs, and looked directly at me. "But your real concern, Ms. Moon, should be more obvious."

"And what would that be?"

"Why did they *really* invite you up here?"

I opened my mouth to answer. The answer, after all, should have been obvious. I had been hired to do a job. To find a killer. Instead, I thought about her question and closed my mouth.

She gave me a weak smile, got up, braced herself for rain to come, and then dashed out.

29.

I was on the phone with Kingsley.

"I assume you need something?" he asked pleasantly, rich humor in his deep voice.

"You assume correctly."

I was in my small bedroom. The door was closed. Allison was cleaning up in the kitchen. Occasionally, my small bedroom window rattled with the passing wind, which shrieked like a living thing. Or a dead thing.

I brought Kingsley up to speed, knowing I sounded insane as I did so, and knowing I sounded, perhaps, even a little hysterical. I was, after all, trapped on an island in the middle of a nasty storm —blustery, my ass—with what appeared to be one equally nasty dark entity. An entity that just might have lured me up here. Successfully, I might add.

Kingsley listened quietly, as he always did. A helluva trait in a man. He occasionally made small, noncommittal noises to let me know he was still there and hearing me—another great trait—and when I was done, he let out some air.

"Wow, Sam."

"Wow what?"

"That's quite a story."

"Thank you for that completely worthless assessment."

"Ouch."

"I'm freaking out over here. Tell me what the hell is going on, please."

"Calm down, Sam—"

"I've got Allison here with me...and I need to keep her safe, too, and I seriously have no clue what's going on."

"Sam, calm down. You didn't let me finish. Yes, that's a wild story, true, but I also think I know what you're up against."

"Oh, thank God."

"Don't thank God me yet, young lady. This thing is about as far away from God as you can imagine. And you and Allison are very much in danger. So much so that I'm heading up there now—"

"Wait, what?"

"I'm literally out the door, Sam."

"Wait, hold on, Kingsley! You can't be serious. Wait, are you in your car?"

"Yes." I heard the zip of a seatbelt being pulled out and a thrumming drone.

"Is that your engine starting?"

"Yes. Sam, this thing is old and evil and absolutely delights in destroying lives."

"Then what does it want with me?"

"I don't know, but it can't be good. Where are your kids?"

"With my sister."

"Good."

"You're scaring me, Kingsley."

"I don't mean to, but this thing is capable of anything...and it wants you for a reason."

"But why did you ask about my kids?"

"I don't know, Sam. But they came to mind."

"I ask because I've been getting a very bad feeling about them, too."

"Then do something about it, Sam. Have your kids and sister—and her whole damn family—stay at my house."

"I don't understand."

"They'll be safe there with Franklin."

"Your butler?"

"Oh, he's much more than a butler, Sam. And trust me, they will be very, very safe."

"So, how will you get here? The ferries are closed, due to the storm."

"I'll figure something out. See you soon, hopefully. Just be safe, Sam, and don't ever underestimate this thing."

"But, what is it?"

There was a small pause before he answered. "I think it just might be the Devil, Sam."

"The Devil?"

"Or something close to it."

30.

I clicked off with Kingsley, and just sat there on the corner of my bed.

The bedroom was small, with a single window to my right that looked out towards the woods beyond. The curtains were open and I watched the rain slanting sideways. They looked like blow-darts from an army of elves.

Or, much more likely, I was losing my friggin' mind.

Did he say the Devil?

As in Satan?

I got up and paced and thought about what I had to do, thought even longer about what I should say to my sister, and then made the call. She picked up on the third ring.

"How's the trip, Sam—"

"Something's wrong."

"What? Is everything okay?"

"I don't think so."

"Sam, what's going on?"

"That's the problem, Mary Lou, I don't know, but I think the kids might be in danger. And you, for that matter."

"You're joking."

"No joke, Mary Lou."

"You're being serious?"

"Sweetie, I am. More than I ever have before. There is something very weird going on, and I've been having a bad feeling about the kids for the past few hours now. I just spoke to Kingsley and he echoed the same feeling."

"Someone might hurt Tammy and Anthony?"

The gut-wrenching feeling gripped me again, tearing at me from the inside. I didn't know if this was a psychic hit or a mother's intuition. "I think so, yes."

"Jesus, Sam. Should I call the police?"

I thought about that, too, then told her to give Detective Sherbet a call at the Fullerton Police Department. To let him know my concerns and where she would be with the kids. She digested that last part.

"You want us to stay at Kingsley's house?"

"Yes."

"With his butler?"

"He's more than a butler."

"Sam, I'm scared."

"So am I."

"What will you do?"

I took in a lot of air and said, "I have no clue."

31.

I next spoke to each of my kids.

I let them know the game plan, let them know that they would be staying over at Uncle Kingsley's house. Tammy snorted. "Don't lie to us, Mom. I read Auntie Louie's mind. She's totally freaked out right now."

I rubbed my forehead and shook my head. It was, after all, impossible to keep anything away from my kids these days. The truth was, I didn't know what, exactly, I was keeping away from them. Only that I needed them somewhere safe. And fast.

I told Tammy to give the phone to her brother and she did. I told Anthony, who was now almost as tall as his sister—his recent growth spurt was alarming, to say the least—that it was his job to protect her.

"I'm on it, Mommy," he said. "If I have to."

"You have to."

"She's kind of a butthead, though."

"Butthead or not, she's still your sister."

"My *ugly* sister, you mean."

"I love you guys," I said, suddenly choked up. God, I even missed their bickering.

"We know, Mommy. You say it all the time. Sheesh."

"Because it's true," I said, drying my eyes.

"But it's *embarrrrrassing*."

"Maybe so, but you need to hear it."

He sighed loudly. "Fine."

"Well?" I asked.

"Well what?"

"You know what I need," I said.

He sighed again, and, ever so softly, whispered, "I guess I love you, too, Mommy."

I would have laughed if the tears didn't come to my eyes again.

He added, "Don't let the bad guys get you, Mommy."

"I won't, baby."

"Bye, Mommy."

And he hung up...and I wiped the tears from my cheeks, and took a deep breath and set my jaw. I had been clenching my hands so tight that my sharp nails had punctured my palms. I opened my hands and watched the small wounds heal before my eyes.

Whoever this motherfucker was, Devil or no

Devil, he was not going to hurt my kids, and he sure as hell wasn't going to keep me from seeing them, again.

Whoever the hell he was.

32.

"I need some air," I said to Allison when I stepped out of my bedroom.

"But it's pouring out there."

I glared at her as she leaped from the couch. "Let me get my jacket."

Soon we were heading away from the bungalows, along a dirt path that led deeper into the surrounding woods. The island itself was sort of long and narrow. The ocean would be only a half mile or so on either side. Although not huge, the island was choked with evergreens and ferns and something called stinging nettles, which Tara had warned us about.

I could give a damn about stinging nettles.

Even though it was only midday, the woods

were dark. But here, under the canopy of evergreens, the storm was nearly non-existent, reduced to only a persistent, howling wind—and a few heavy drops.

The path before us was mostly dirt. I could see deer tracks in the mud, and what was surely a dog's tracks, although they could have been coyotes. I frowned at that. I didn't think coyotes were on the island.

Allison looked miserable and cold. She buried her face in her oversized jacket. Myself, I was wearing only a light windbreaker. I was fairly certain my body temperature was even lower than the surrounding wind and rain.

I veered off on a smaller side-trail, and there we found a massive tree with the widest trunk I'd ever seen. I stopped and turned to Allison, who'd been following with her head mostly ducked, doing her best not to trip over the many exposed tree roots.

"We need to talk," I said.

"I figured that."

"We might be in some deep shit."

"I figured that, too."

"I just talked to Kingsley."

"The werewolf."

"Yes."

"Your ex-boyfriend."

"Yes."

"You do realize that a vampire dating a werewolf is a little too...clichéd?"

"Allison..."

"Sorry, sorry...you were saying?"

"There's some scary shit going on here. Kingsley's coming out."

"What? Why?"

"He thinks I'm in way over my head."

"Sam, from what you've told me, you've faced some crazy shit."

"Maybe none crazier than this."

"Even crazier than me?" asked Allison.

I laughed. I needed that. The tree branches high above us swished and swayed violently. Never had I seen trees like this. So tall, so beautiful. Now as I stood there in the forest, I noticed little balls of light moving about. These bright balls stopped often at plants and at the bases of trees. I watched one stop near a toadstool.

Allison caught my thoughts, and said, "I see those lights, too, sometimes. At parks, and sometimes on my balcony garden at home."

"What are they?"

"If I had to guess, I would say fairies."

I snorted.

"Scoffs the vampire," said Allison, shaking her head. "You, better than most, should know that there are some strange things under the sun...or under the moon."

"But fairies?" I asked. "With little wings? Like Tinker Bell?"

"Think of them as nature spirits, Sammie. And no little wings, as far as I can tell. Just peaceful, loving entities that tend to Mother Earth."

I watched the lights flit around the forest some more, dozens of them. Many dozens. They were often the same size, each no bigger than a tennis ball, and their colors ranged from light blue to burning white. One sidled up next to us, slipped between my legs and moved over to a dying fern. It moved carefully over the plant, touching down on each outstretched branch, and then moved on. I sensed, on some level, that it was comforting the dying plant. Weird, yes, but I found the gesture oddly touching.

"So, what do we do, Sam?" asked Allison after a moment or two.

"*We* don't do anything. *I* need to find out what the hell is going on here. You're going to stay in the bungalow—and stay out of trouble."

She was about to protest when she saw the look in my eye. "Fine, I'll stay out of trouble, but I want you to know that I'm lodging a formal complaint."

"Duly noted," I said.

"So, then, what are you going to do?" she asked, ducking as a particularly large glob of water splattered on her nose.

"I'm going to have a little talk with our client."

"Tara? But isn't she one of them?"

"Exactly," I said, and turned and headed back through the forest, with Allison stumbling and cursing behind me.

33.

As I left Allison in the bungalow, confident that she would be safe for the time being, trusting my inner alarm system—and my own gut feeling—I paused just outside the door.

As rain battered me, I decided to change plans, at least for the time being.

Instead of talking to Tara, I hung a right and headed back into the forest, and found a side trail that I had seen from high above the night before. The trail, wide at first, soon narrowed considerably. I didn't know much about forests or hiking or even trails, but I figured this to be a game trail.

I continued on, pushing through massive ferns that seemed almost prehistoric. Thorny raspberry bushes were in abundance as well, all filled with juicy berries that probably tasted heavenly. The trail angled up, as I knew it would.

Stinging nettles snagged my jeans as I carefully stepped over fat banana slugs—and even the occasional toadstool. I marveled at the mushrooms that clung to moist tree trunks. Nature at its weirdest. Water dripped seemingly everywhere. Lightning suddenly flashed above, zigzagging through the treetops, followed by an angry grumbling of thunder.

I continued on, slipping once or twice in the sloshing mud, winding my way up the trail that would lead to the highest point of the island.

Soon, as the trees opened and the wind and rain lashed me violently, I found myself on a steep switchback trail that afforded a majestic view of the manor far below. The trail soon led to a rounded rock dome high above the island. I didn't know if it had a name, but I called it Dome Rock.

Rain drove straight into my face, down inside my jacket collar. I didn't mind the rain at all. It made me feel alive. Human. Normal. Rain didn't judge or discriminate. Rain fell on everyone...mortal or immortal. Living or dead.

Or some of us in-between.

I slipped and slid my way over the moss-covered rock and soon looked out over the Puget Sound, to distant islands and churning seas. It was so beautiful and epic and alive that it was nearly impossible to believe that a family was being terrorized by a body-jumping demon.

Nearly.
I knew one thing, though: I wanted answers.
And I knew just where to find them.
God.

34.

I sat cross-legged at the apex of the dome, completely exposed to the storm.

At times, the wind blew so hard that I thought it might lift me up and blow me off the rock mound. But it didn't, try as it might. Instead it tugged and pulled at me like an angry thing, as I remained seated and focused.

My eyes were closed tight; my hands rested on my knees.

The wind thundered over my exposed ears. Yes, my hood was down. I didn't want any barrier between me and God. I breathed in and out, slowly. Now, the wind blew even harder, rocking me further and, in the far distance, I heard the pounding of the surf against the rock cliffs.

I continued breathing, slowly, deliberately, deeply.

It took a minute or two of focused concentration, but soon enough, I felt a sensation of rising up, as if I'd entered a tube of some sort. A glass tube, because in my mind's eye I could see myself rising up. But, interestingly, not so much rising above the earth. No. Instead, I sensed myself rising up through what appeared to be levels.

Dimensions.

How I knew this, I didn't know. But the word felt right. Yes, I was rising up through the dimensions, even as the rain hit me full in the face. The sensation of being wet and cold seemed to be happening to someone else. Certainly not me...after all, I was rising, rising.

Rising...

The dimensions swept past me. On many of them I sensed entities, or beings, watching me, observing me while I came and went. Spiritual beings, I knew, highly evolved beings that existed in realms that we, as humans, could not comprehend...and yet, I sped past even them.

Higher and higher.

Until...

I was back. Not above the Earth, or even above the Universe. I was *outside* of the Universe. Outside of space and time. I was observing creation as God would have. As God did so now.

Welcome back, Samantha Moon, came a thought deep inside my head. No, not exactly in my head.

All around me, vibrating through me.

I sensed that I existed in the space between space, and it was a concept that was difficult for me to understand.

You are doing fine, Samantha Moon.

Thank you. You are doing fine, too, from what I can gather.

There was a gentle laugh inside me. *Kind of you to say, Sam. Do you mind if I call you Sam?*

You're God, you can call me anything you want.

More gentle laughter. God, I was discovering, had a nice sense of humor. *I understand that you think that, Sam. But I am, more accurately, the Source.*

Source?

The Source of life in this universe.

I see, I thought. *I think. That's still pretty much God to me.*

I will not argue the point, Sam. Either way, it's a pleasure to have your company.

I sensed the vastness, the emptiness, the peace.

Do you ever feel lonely out here? I asked.

Your question implies that I might find myself alone.

Well, yes, I guess. Are there many others like you? Other Sources?

There are a handful of us, yes.

How many?

Twelve, to be exact.

And from where do the twelve originate?

Exactly that, Sam. From the Origin.

And what, exactly, is the Origin?

My Creator.

I see, I thought. *And you are my Creator?*

You are my creation, yes.

And what do the other twelve Sources do?

They watch over their own multiverses, of course.

Of course. And why did the Origin create twelve of you?

To learn more about itself.

And why did you create me?

So that I can learn more about myself.

And thus, what? Report back to the Origin? I asked.

You are correct, Sam.

I thought about this as the rain and wind pummeled my physical body a universe away, as I gazed out over the slowly-moving cosmos that rotated around a galactic center of some sort.

That's pretty heavy, I thought.

It's as heavy or light as you want it to be. But, yes, I understand that these are new concepts for you in the physical world.

Is there evil? I asked suddenly.

There is the potential for others to show you the opposite of light, yes.

I had a sudden insight, sudden clarity. I wondered if this insight came from the Source.

The darkness is necessary to appreciate the light, I said.

Well said, Sam.

Can darkness ever destroy light?

There was a slight pause before the voice vibrated through my being again: *Remember this always, Sam: A small match can illuminate the darkest room.*

I got the meaning and felt myself nod way, way back there on that rock dome, high above Skull Island.

So, I should never fear darkness, I thought.

Live in light, Samantha, but acknowledge the darkness.

For without darkness, there cannot be light.

Very good, Sam.

Is there a Devil? I asked suddenly.

There was a long pause. *You are asking if there is an entity that delights in causing mischief, who tortures souls for all eternity, who causes the good to falter, and the bad to be worse?*

Well, yes.

No, Sam. No such entity exists.

I nodded. Perhaps here in space, or perhaps back on the dome, I said, *I have a question about a group of beings I have come across, one such being is, in fact, residing within me, and undoubtedly hearing this very conversation.*

Maybe she needs to hear this conversation, Samantha. Maybe you are her answer, too.

I don't understand.

Maybe you are her way back to the light.

I never thought of that. I paused, formulating my thoughts. *I feel she is evil.*

She—and others like her—have certainly made choices that might appear evil.

But they are not evil? I asked.

They operate out of fear, Sam. Fear of moving on, fear of giving up power, fear of retribution. They are, quite simply, misinformed.

Misinformed about what?

That life is eternal, that I am eternal. That they are eternal. That power is temporary, that love is everlasting.

Is there evil?

There is no evil, Samantha Moon.

Lightning flashed in the heavens above...until I realized that it had flashed directly above my body. I was about to ask another question, until I felt myself slipping back...or down through the dimensions. As I slipped down, down, God's words sang through me and around me.

Love is everlasting.

I opened my eyes and looked out over stormy seas and wondered again if I'd completely lost my mind.

35.

As I hiked back from the dome, still reeling from yet another encounter with God—or, perhaps more accurately, the Source—I sent a text message to Tara Thurman:

We need to talk.

Her reply came a few minutes later, as I slid and skated down the muddy trail.

I know.

Meet me at my bungalow in twenty minutes.

Where are you?

Nature walk, I texted and shoved my phone in my hip pocket before the rain could short-circuit something. I might be able to do a lot of things, but magically fix my iPhone wasn't one of them.

Back at the bungalow, I let Allison know we

were expecting a guest. Allison read my mind, shook her head, and went immediately into the kitchen and took out a big carving knife.

"She's one of *them*, Sammie," she said, slipping it inside her waistband, and then yelping loudly when the point bit her.

I snickered and reminded her that the entity, as far as we knew, could only jump from one body at a time.

"Well, we don't know that for sure, Sam. In fact, we know very little about it."

"Which is why I want to talk to Tara."

Allison still didn't like it, except this time she gingerly slipped the knife inside her waistband. I chuckled and took a shower. Showers were still one of my few great pleasures in this new life of mine, and I reveled in the warmth it provided, always reluctant to leave. Even after the shower was long off, I stood there briefly in the stall, the heat and steam, and watched the water drip down my still-pale skin. Pale and flawless, granted.

No, I thought. *Pale and dead.*

I threw on my last pair of dry jeans, then tossed my sopping-wet clothes in the bungalow's washer. I'd just turned it on and was toweling my hair when a gentle rap came on the front door.

As of someone gently rapping, I thought, thinking of the Edgar Allan Poe poem, *rapping at my chamber door.*

***

As I reached for the door, I mentally reminded Allison to guard her thoughts. She understood...and reached down and adjusted the knife at her hip. I might have detected a small spot of blood appearing through her jeans where the point had poked her.

I next remembered the words of the Source: *They operate out of fear, Sam. Fear of moving on, fear of giving up power, fear of retribution. They are, quite simply, misinformed.*

Misinformed or not, the being that possessed the Thurmans was, I suspected, desperate and powerful. A hell of a dangerous combination. But I would not fear it, whatever it was.

The smallest match can illuminate the darkest room.

I opened the door, stepped aside, and let the Devil in.

36.

Tara, of course, didn't look like the Devil.

Or a highly evolved dark master, for that matter. In fact, other than looking wet and cold, she looked exactly as I'd remembered her: young, fresh-faced, alert, alive. Not pale and gaunt. Not vampiric.

It's because he's not a vampire, Allison said. *Not quite.*

I nodded minutely as I invited Tara to have a seat. She did so at the small kitchen table. I asked if she wanted Allison to make her some coffee. Tara shook her head—and just missed the nasty look Allison shot me.

I considered how to broach the subject of her family, and decided to dive right in. "I've heard about the family curse," I said.

Tara, who was wearing a cute pair of tight jeans and bright red rain boots lined with rabbit fur, snapped her head up. The black, vaporous thread that wound through her aura pulsated a little.

He's listening, I thought. How I knew this, I didn't know, but it seemed obvious now.

"Who told you?"

"That's not important now. What can you tell me about it?"

Her own once-vibrant aura seemed to shrink a little, a sign that she was going within, closing herself off to me. "Sam, it's really quite silly."

"From what I heard, it didn't sound silly," I said. "It sounded dangerous."

The black thread began rotating slowly through her aura now, weaving in and out. Tara held my gaze briefly, and then looked away. I felt her fear.

"It's really not something I want to talk about," she said. "Also, I don't see what this has to do with why I hired you."

"Why are you afraid?" I asked.

She looked at me, then at the door. I reached out and took her hand. As I did so, the black, ethereal snake swelled briefly and circled even faster, weaving in and out, watching me carefully. Yes, I sensed it watching me.

"You're not leaving," I said.

"Hey, let go."

"I know about the curse, Tara," I said, squeezing her even tighter, but not so tight as to hurt her. Tight enough for her to know she wasn't going anywhere. After all, I was going to have to get through decades of fear and confusion. "I know about your great-grandfather, and I know what he brought upon your family."

She fought me briefly, but to no avail. As I held her hand, I got psychic hit after psychic hit.

"No," she said. "It's just a silly superstition—"

"You and I both know it's not a superstition. You and I both know that something dark and angry and hungry has entered your lives. Something that will never leave."

"You're crazy, Sam—"

"You feel it in you, you feel it when it overcomes you. You feel it make you say things, do things, want things. You thought you were crazy. You thought all of you were crazy. But it's in you. You understand that now. It's in all of you. In your blood. Like a parasite. A leech. A disease."

"You're crazy, Sam."

"I'm not crazy. And neither are you."

Tears welled up in her eyes. She looked over at Allison, then back at me. "Why are you doing this? What's the matter with you? I hired you to find answers to my grandfather's death."

"And I am," I said. "But ask yourself: Why did you hire me? Why me, out of hundreds of other private investigators?"

"I live in southern California. I...I liked your ad."

"You live in Los Angeles, nowhere near me."

"Your ad..." she mumbled.

"I see," I said. "And why were you looking for a private investigator in Orange County?"

"I don't—" She paused, fumbling for words. The black snake swirling faster and faster, weaving, in and out...

"You don't know why, do you?" I said.

"I don't—"

"You don't know why because *it* compelled you to call me, to hire me."

"Sam, please—"

"How did you know Detective Sherbet?"

"I didn't know him."

Something very much wanted me to have Sherbet's recommendation. I rarely, if ever, turned anyone away who had first come from Sherbet. Something wanted to guarantee that I would take the case.

"It compelled you to seek him out, didn't it?"

"Yes—"

My hands shot out and took both of hers this time. I dug my nail deep into her skin, making blood contact. She gasped, and in a flash, I saw it now, saw how it worked, saw how it used her and the others. The secret manipulation, down through the ages. I saw how it rarely, if ever, revealed its plans to them. It simply manipulated, used them. Like a sick puppet master. Mostly it left them alone. Mostly. That is, until it needed something from them—or wanted them to do something for it. In this case, it had compelled Tara to call me and hire me. But she did not know why. It had kept its reasons to itself.

I released her as she recoiled, rubbing her now-bleeding hands, shocked and clearly horrified. But I had seen what I needed to see. There had, of course, been something else I had seen. Something very, very strange.

"Tell me about the digging," I said.

The black snake had swollen to nearly twice its usual size. The entity was here, but hadn't quite taken over Tara fully. No, it was surveying the damage, assessing what needed to be done, if anything.

"It makes us dig," she said finally. "On the north end of the island."

"Dig for what?"

"I don't know."

"But it's searching for something?"

"Yes."

"Is that why you were gone yesterday?"

She looked at me with pleading eyes. I saw the torment in her soul, felt the anguish in her heart. I knew the source of her pain: the entity had taken so much from her and her family.

"Yes," she said. "It doesn't tell us what it's looking for."

"Us?"

"Yes. Mostly it uses Edwin and me. When he's resting, I take over."

"What part of the island, exactly?"

Tara shook her head. "I...I can't say."

"It won't let you say, you mean?"

She looked at me with pleading eyes. And nodded.

"Tara, would you like for me to remove this entity from your lives?"

Her mouth dropped open to speak, but she didn't, couldn't. The swirling black snake was so thick now, so dense, that it almost appeared real. The entity, I knew, had just taken her over.

The son of a bitch.

Still, Tara nodded. A very small nod. It was all she could do against the will of the entity who, I knew, presently possessed her. Tara wanted help. Badly.

Now she stood slowly and smiled down at me. The same creepy smile I had seen on her before. "You cannot win, Samantha Moon," she said evenly, except it wasn't her. "Not against me. Not against us."

And she turned and left the bungalow.

37.

"That was so creepy," said Allison.

"As hell," I said.

"It allowed her to give you that information about the digging," said Allison.

"I know."

"It could have stopped her earlier, but didn't," said Allison. "Which means..."

"Which means it wanted me to know about the digging."

"But why?"

"I don't know," I said.

I nodded absently. I couldn't stop thinking about the desperate look in Tara's eyes, even as she was compelled to say the words that came out of her mouth at the end, even as she was compelled to get up and leave.

I shuddered as my cell phone rang.

Secure line. Detective Sherbet, no doubt. I picked up immediately.

"Sam, it's Sherbet."

"I would never have guessed."

"No jokes, Sam. Someone tried to break into your home last night."

"My kids—"

"Are safe with me. I'm here at Kingsley's home, if you want to call it that—"

"What happened, Detective?"

"A neighbor reported the break-in. Nothing was stolen, as far as we know." He paused. "But they really weren't looking to steal anything, were they, Sam?"

"I don't think so," I said.

"What were they looking for, Samantha? Be straight with me."

I thought of Kingsley words, words that still made me feel sick to my stomach.

"My kids, I think," I said.

"Why?"

"I don't know yet."

"Christ, you get into some weird shit." He paused. "Sam, there's something else."

My heart thumped hard. "What?"

"Kingsley's rather, um, interesting manservant."

"Butler," I said.

"Whatever. Frankie or whatever his name is, claimed to have seen someone lurking outside

Kingsley's house this morning—"

"Shit."

"Sam, what the devil is going on?"

I gave him a glimpse of my thoughts, even long distance, and I sensed him shaking his head. "You have got to be kidding me," he said.

"No."

"That's some weird shit."

"Detective, I think it's important that you take my kids somewhere else."

"Where?"

I thought hard about that. "Somewhere I don't know. Somewhere safe."

"Somewhere you don't know? What the devil are you..." And then Sherbet, the only other human being besides Allison who was privy to my thoughts, finally caught on. "I understand. I mean, I really don't understand. In fact, I'm fairly certain I'm going batshit crazy. But, yeah, I think I understand."

"You do?" I said urgently.

"Yeah, you don't want me to tell you where I'm taking the kids because..." he paused, no doubt searching for words.

"Yes," I said, finishing for him, "because the thing inside me is listening."

38.

"We need to know why this entity brought me up here," I said when I'd hung up with Sherbet.

"And why it wants your kids," chimed in Allison.

Another very cold chill went through me. I began pacing in the bungalow. Who had come to my house? Who was outside of Kingsley's house? Why did they want my kids?

"I think we know who," said Allison, somehow following my frantic thoughts. "I'm certain the Thurman clan reaches far and wide."

I sat on the arm of the leather sofa, ran both hands through my hair. My too-thick hair. Never was my hair this thick when I was mortal.

"He controls them all," continued Allison,

"anyone with a drop of Thurman blood."

"Jesus," I said. "So how do we stop him?"

"That," said Allison, "is why you make the big bucks."

"Great," I said, and thought again about the image I'd received from Tara: that of her and Edwin digging on the north side of the island.

"A good place to start," said Allison, following along. "Except if she doesn't even know what they're digging for, what makes you think we would know?"

"That," I said, "is why they invented the Internet."

"I thought they invented the Internet for porn?"

"That, too," I said. "Grab your laptop, and let's see what we can find."

"Yes, ma'am," said my new friend, and did just that.

***

It didn't take us long to find something.

"A shipwreck," said Allison, pointing to screen. "Over a hundred years ago, right off the north side of Skull Island. Okay, we are definitely venturing into Scooby-Doo territory here."

"Except Scooby-Doo and the gang didn't deal with a body-jumping demon who's after me and my kids. Read the article."

She did.

In 1896, a shipping vessel hit rough waters just

north of Skull Island. Most of the crew of fifteen survived, except for the captain who went down, proverbially, with the ship. The remaining fourteen crew members, via life rafts, eventually washed up onto Skull Island, where they were soon rescued.

"Weird and cool all rolled into one," said Allison. "But I don't see how that helps us."

I didn't see it either. "What's the name of the historian quoted in the article?"

"Abraham Gunthrie, college professor from Western Washington University in a city called Bellingham."

"Where's Bellingham?"

She brought up the city and college on Google Maps. Bellingham was north of here, about an hour away as the eagle flies. Or, in my case, as the giant vampire bat flies. I bumped Allison rudely out of her seat and, while she protested and rubbed her bruised hip, I brought up one of my proprietary websites and entered in my username and password. A few clicks later and I had the information I needed. The professor's home address.

"That's kinda scary how fast you can do that."

"I use my powers for good," I said. "Mostly."

"You do realize that the storm is even worse. No one is leaving or coming to the island."

"Not everyone," I said. I logged off the site, got up and began packing myself a weatherproof bag.

39.

I was flying.

Through wind and rain and lightning. Kinda like the mailman, only scary as hell.

Below, the gray, churning sea spread far and wide. The vague shape of a distant land mass was my target. Lightning appeared around me, sometimes just barely missing me. I wondered what it would feel like to be struck by lightning. Probably hurt like hell. Would I plunge from the sky, to sink to the bottom of the ocean?

Maybe. Sinking to the bottom of the ocean didn't concern me much, since I had little use for my lungs. In fact, I quite enjoyed plunging into the water every now and then and gliding like a great manta ray.

Hanging from one of my scary-looking talons was my favorite Samsonite carry-on bag. I continued about a thousand feet over the churning ocean, buffeted by winds that threatened to knock me off course—threatened, but never succeeding. My wings were powerful in this form. I was powerful in this form. It would take a lot more than a gale-force wind to knock me down.

Shortly, I came upon a rocky shoreline and a few scattered homes. I followed a meandering road that wound along the edge of the land, affording, undoubtedly, wonderful views of the ocean.

More homes appeared as the road angled inland. And there, through the driving rain, was the sparkling city of Bellingham. I circled above it within the clouds, looking for a good spot to land, and found one in a park near the university.

I alighted smoothly upon a bench because, in this form, I seemed to prefer landing *on* something —rocks, tree limbs, park benches—which I could never quite figure out.

Must be the bird of prey in me.

I tucked my wings in, and once again saw the vision of the woman in the flame—and soon, a curvy but toned mother of two, was squatting naked on the same park bench, a Samsonite carry-on bag looped around her ankle.

Sometimes it's fun to be me.

Weird, but fun.

40.

After dressing and hailing a cab, I was soon standing outside of Professor Abraham Gunthrie's quaint little home.

A typical Washington home, I discovered: clapboard siding, cute herbal garden, and a stone path through roses. There was a wooden wraparound porch with views of the University and his equally charming neighbors' homes. I wondered if he ever suspected a creature of the night would be descending upon his idyllic world.

Probably not. Then again, he probably never expected a private eye to come knocking, either.

Which is exactly what I did. Three times, loud enough to be heard throughout the small home. I watched a squirrel make a mad dash out into the storm and cross the manicured lawn. About halfway, it paused, no doubt regretting its decision to leave its cozy, acorn-filled nook somewhere high in the tree. Finally, it continued on, running and hopping alternately.

As it disappeared from view, I heard footsteps creak across a wooden floor and approach the front door. I already had my business card in hand as I waited.

The man who opened the door was older, as I knew he would be. Abraham Gunthrie sported a Van Dyke goatee, pointed at the end, and some errant ear hair. His eyebrows looked bushy enough for that squirrel I'd just seen to hide its acorns in.

"May I help you?" he asked. His voice was stronger than he looked. I briefly imagined him standing before his students, his deep voice easily reaching the back rows.

"Are you Professor Gunthrie?" I asked.

"For you, I'll be anyone you want."

Whoa. There was still some pep to his step. I smiled, perhaps bigger than I'd intended. He smiled, too, and showed me a lot of coffee-stained teeth.

"Professor Gunthrie, I'm a private investigator and I'd like to ask you a few questions about a shipwreck on Skull Island."

He blinked, absorbed what I said, then accepted my proffered business card, which he looked over carefully. He said, "You sound very official, Detective Moon." He winked. "I supposed I'd better invite you in, then."

"Thank you," I said.

And as I stepped past him, the old guy might have—*just might have*—checked out my ass.

The interior was as warm and cozy as the exterior promised. A fire burned energetically in the fireplace. Pictures of kids and grandkids adorned the wall. An elderly woman was in many of the pictures. The photos were of his deceased wife, I knew, because her spirit was presently standing in the room as well, watching us silently.

I'd gotten used to such spirits. Mostly, they didn't expect me to see them, and mostly, I pretended not to see them. In this case, I gave her a small nod and smile. The woman, who was composed of hundreds, if not thousands, of particles of white light, seemed to do a double take, then slowly nodded toward me.

"Beautiful home," I said, noting the maritime theme mixed with the family photos.

"Made more beautiful now," he said, winking at me. Slightly embarrassed, I looked over at his departed wife. She simply shook her head and appeared to chuckle, although it was hard to tell because her features weren't fully formed.

"Well, thank you," I said.

"Would you like some tea, Ms. Moon?"

"Water would be great."

"I can do water. Have a seat." He gestured toward a well-worn couch with a colorful afghan blanket thrown over the back.

Professor Gunthrie shuffled off into the kitchen,

where I next heard water dispense from a cooler. Shortly, he returned with two glasses of water, which he set before us on little doily coasters at the coffee table. I sipped from my glass politely. He seemed pleased. In fact, he seemed pleased just to have any company at all. Even vampire company.

A model of a clipper ship stretched across the length of the coffee table. Tammy and Anthony would have broken that in two hours. Maybe one hour. Maybe instantly.

"So, what can I do for you, Ms. Moon?" he asked, glancing at my business card again. He seemed impressed. Or maybe that was wishful thinking on my part.

"I'm looking into a shipwreck that occurred on Skull Island in the late nineteenth century."

"*The Sea Merchant,*" he said, nodding.

"What can you tell me about that shipwreck that, well, didn't make it to the papers?"

"Or onto the Internet?" he asked, winking.

"That, too," I said, grinning.

"Perhaps the most interesting would have been that *The Sea Merchant* was transporting a small amount of treasure."

"Treasure?"

"Of sorts," he said, and drank long and hard from his own glass of water. "A man by the name of Archibald Maximus lost his fortune. Lots of gold, and other valuables. Apparently, he was quite the collector. Are you okay, Ms. Moon?"

Had I any color in my cheeks, I'm sure it would

have drained. As it was, I'm fairly certain my mouth might have dropped open. I tried to recover valiantly. "Any idea what this treasure might have contained?"

"Gold, from the reports. Not a king's ransom, granted, but certainly enough to keep the treasure hunters searching, which they continue to do to this day."

"I see," I said. "Thank you."

"Is there anything else I can do for you, Ms. Moon? Would you like something to eat? I just made a wonderful quiche—"

"No, thank you. I appreciate your help."

I stood to leave. He stood, too. "Do you have to leave so soon?" He was lonely and I knew it.

"I'm afraid so."

He looked briefly pained, and then nodded. As he walked me to the front door, I reached out to the female spirit watching us from the corner of the room.

"Your wife is here with you, Professor Gunthrie," I said.

"Excuse me?"

"I'm a sort of...medium. Your wife is here, in this room."

"Why would you say—"

"Her name is Helen, and she says she will always love you."

He blinked rapidly, and actually looked toward the area where the spirit of his deceased wife was presently watching us. "Well, you're a private eye,

I'm sure you could have found that out—"

"She wants to thank you for planting the roses in her honor. She knows you think of her every time you see them."

His mouth opened, and then closed. He tried again, and then closed it again.

I continued. "She loves you now more than ever, and is with you always."

"Samantha...I don't understand."

"It's okay if you don't understand, Professor. She wants me to tell you that when you lie in bed and feel all alone that you are never alone. Not ever. She's lying right there with you, in spirit."

He rubbed his eyes. "I...I feel her, sometimes."

"When you see her in your dreams, she wants you to know that's her, coming to you."

"I dream of her all the time."

I smiled sweetly at him. "And there's something else she wants me to give you."

"What?"

I leaned in and kissed him ever-so-softly on the corner of his mouth. "That's from her."

He broke down for a minute or two and I waited, checking my watch. I nodded toward Helen, who had drifted over and was now standing nearby.

She thanked me, and I smiled at her, then squeezed Professor's Gunthrie's hand, and left him weeping in the doorway.

Alone. In theory.

41.

I was back on Skull Island.

Total elapsed time was just over an hour. I found Allison where I'd left her: in her bedroom lying with the steak knife clutched in her hand. Her bone-white hand. Yes, I'd felt bad leaving her, but trusted our psychic connection to alert me should she be in any danger.

"What took you so long?" she asked, setting the knife aside after virtually prying her fingers open. "I thought super bats made great time."

I ignored her; instead, I filled her in on what I'd learned.

"And who's Archibald Maximus?" she asked.

"He's a librarian at Cal State Fullerton."

"The University?"

"Yes."

"What is he, like 215 years old?"

Her math, I suspected, was dubious. I said, "No. He looks younger than you, although that's not hard to do."

"Mean, Samantha Moon," she said. "Very mean. Is he a vampire, too?"

"No. Not quite. He's something else."

She read my thoughts. "An ascended master?"

"Or a warrior of the light," I said. "He's here to counterbalance the darkness."

"Is he single?"

"Allison..."

"Sorry, sorry. So, what does all this mean?"

"I don't know yet," I said.

"He obviously survived the shipwreck, since only the captain died."

"Right," I said.

"And he was transporting a treasure."

"Right again," I said.

"What kind of treasure would a warrior of the light have?" asked Allison. "I mean, isn't he supposed to be above material wealth and all that?"

"Maybe," I said, and thought of the simple young man I'd met a few times now working in the Occult Room at Cal State Fullerton, a young man who wasn't so young after all. A young man who had, quite remarkably, reversed my son's vampirism, using the first of four powerful medallions.

Medallions he had shown me in a book.

Medallions that were created, he'd said, to counter the effects of vampirism, although he had told me nothing more.

Allison had been following my train of thoughts, seeing my memory as I reviewed it.

"Four medallions," she said, commenting on the book Archibald had once shown me of the four golden discs.

"Yes," I said.

"And you have had two of them?"

"Yes."

"Aren't these, like, rare?"

"Well, there's only four of them."

"And one of them is presently on you—"

"*In* me," I corrected, and showed her the circular-shaped scar along my upper chest.

"Gotcha. And easy on the vampire cleavage, Sam. Kinda gross." She faked a shiver. "How did you get the first one?"

"It was sort of hand-delivered to me."

I gave her the image of the hunky, blond-haired vampire hunter who'd posed as a UPS deliveryman. She nodded. "And why did he deliver the medallion to you?"

"I'm not entirely sure."

"Sam, perhaps you are not seeing this, so let me spell it out for you: there are only four of these bad boys in the whole wide world."

I waited. She waited.

"Well?" she asked, exasperated.

"Well, what?"

She rolled her eyes and got up and stood in front of me. "Sam, somehow you are *attracting* these medallions."

"*Pshaw*," I said, blowing her off. "Only a coincidence."

"Is it, Sam? And now you are on an island where, quite possibly, one of the medallions is hidden."

"That's a leap," I said.

"Is it? The same entity, the same warrior of the light, lost his treasure over a hundred years ago, a treasure that has never been found—"

"Because it sank off the coast. It's buried in muck."

"Or is it?" asked Allison. She was on a roll. "There were fourteen survivors, Sam. They obviously had life rafts of some sort. How easily could our friend Archibald Maximus—the same guy, mind you, who first showed you the book containing the four medallions—how easily could he have hidden his treasure here on this island?"

"You're crazy," I said. "There's no evidence of the treasure being hidden on the island."

"And there's no evidence of it ever being found, either. Didn't the professor say that divers have been looking for it for decades? Well, maybe they're looking in the *wrong place*. Maybe they should be looking here, on this island—where, I might add, this entity friend of ours is compelling Tara and Edwin to dig endlessly."

I opened my mouth to speak. There was a sort

of insane logic to what she was saying.

"Insane?" she echoed, reading my thoughts.

"Kinda crazy, kiddo," I said. "But what makes you think Archibald even had one of the medallions?"

"I don't know, but it makes sense. A treasure, Sam. A treasure. The medallion would be considered treasure, wouldn't it? Besides, what else would the entity have Edwin and Tara looking for? The family doesn't exactly need a few crappy gold coins."

"I could use a few crappy gold coins."

"Me, too," said Allison. "My point is this: there is a very good chance the third medallion is here, on this island."

"Then why lure me up here?"

"Isn't it obvious, Sam?"

"No."

"The entity—and now me—thinks that you can help it find it."

"Now *that's* crazy."

"Maybe, maybe not. Remember, Sam, you have possessed two prior medallions. By this point, it might be desperate."

"Fine. Then what does it want with my kids?"

And just as the question escaped my lips, I knew the answer. Allison, in tune with my own thoughts, gasped.

"One of the medallions is in you," she said. "And the other medallion..."

"Is in my son," I said grimly.

"Didn't Archibald break down the other medallion into some sort of potion?"

I nodded, feeling so sick that I could vomit. A potion that my son drank. "Yes."

"A medallion which reversed your son's vampirism?" said Allison.

"Mostly."

"So, in effect, one medallion is in you, and one is in him, and the third..."

"Might just be on this island," I said, and held my stomach, thinking of my son.

"But why does he want the medallions?"

"I don't know."

It was at that moment that a God-awful loud wolf-howl blasted through the blowing wind.

Allison jumped. "Jesus, was that a wolf?"

"Yes," I said, feeling some relief.

"Here on the island? I thought there were no predators."

"Not of the mortal kind," I said. "Get dressed."

42.

We found him in the back woods, dripping wet.

"Don't say it, Sam," said Kingsley.

"Say what?" I asked innocently enough.

"Anything about a wet dog."

"I would never say anything about you looking just like a wet dog caught out in the rain."

Kingsley shook his great, shaggy head and looked over at Allison. Only someone oblivious would miss the way his eyes reflected amber. Damn beautiful eyes.

Yes, I used to enjoy staring into those eyes, especially on nights when my sister had the kids. I had just been falling in love with the big oaf, when he decided to unzip his fly at the wrong time.

Bastard.

"Don't look at me that way, Sam," he said.

"What way?"

"Like you want to take a chainsaw to my balls."

Allison snorted. She was, I sensed, quite smitten with Kingsley Fulcrum. No surprise there. Hard to resist someone who stood six and a half feet tall, and had shoulders wide enough to see from outer space.

Down girl, I said to her telepathically.

I think I'm in love.

No, you're not.

To Kingsley, I said, "I'll add that to my to-do list. Might teach you a lesson."

"If it keeps you from hating me, then do it."

"You two are funny," said Allison.

"Who's the broad?" asked Kingsley, jabbing a thick thumb in her direction.

"Broad?" she laughed. "Do people really talk that way?"

"They do when they're almost a hundred years old."

"Sam!" snapped Kingsley.

"She knows everything, you big ape."

"I've never met a werewolf before," said Allison, stepping around him. Kingsley, I noted, lifted his upper lip in what might have been an irritated snarl. "Are they always as big as you?" she asked.

"Sam..." growled Kingsley. His wet hair hung below the collar of his soaking-wet jacket and jeans. He was also—I could hardly believe it—barefoot.

"There are no secrets between Sam and I," said Allison. "At least not many. We're blood sisters, so to speak."

Kingsley growled again and shook his head, just like a wet dog. Allison and I squealed and took cover.

"Oops, sorry," he said, and I caught his impish grin.

"You can trust her," I said, wiping my face. "It's *you* who I can't trust."

"Low blow, Sam. I came all the way out here to help you, not take abuse."

"You deserve some abuse," I said.

"Fine," he said. "Then are we done?"

"Maybe," I said. "And that reminds me...how did you get out here? No ferries or boats are out in this weather."

"I can still swim, Sam."

"Dog paddle?"

"Ha-ha."

"Okay, I'm done," I said, until his words hit me full force. "Jesus, did you really swim?"

"Not all of us can fly, Sam."

I recalled the churning waves, the white caps. The sea was angry. Kingsley, I knew, was no ordinary man. Or even an ordinary werewolf. Mortal or immortal, few could have made that swim, especially in these conditions.

"We need to get you dry," I said.

"No," he said. "We need to keep you safe. What's going on? Bring me up to speed."

And so we did, there in the forest, while the big hulk of a man occasionally wrung out his hair, all while the treetops swayed violently. Finally, when we were done, he said, "I agree with Allison."

She beamed.

I said, "What part?"

"All of it. The medallion must be here. It's the only thing that makes sense. And I think we should beat the bastard to it."

"What do you mean?" I asked. I was pretty sure my eyes narrowed suspiciously.

"Let's find the medallion first."

"And then do what with it?" I asked.

"We'll cross the bridge when we get there."

I opened my mouth to protest. I wasn't as entirely convinced as my two friends—one of whom was, of course, an ex-boyfriend and just barely in the "friend" category. Still, I couldn't think of a reason to protest. Hell, maybe they were right. Maybe I was, somehow, attached to the medallions.

If it's even here on the island, I thought.

It's here, thought Allison. *I'm sure of it. I'm psychic, too, remember?"*

I sighed and nodded, and was about to suggest that we go back for shovels when Allison pointed out that there was probably equipment on the other side of the island. I nodded again, recalling my flight over the north end of the land mass. Yes, I had seen what appeared to be sheds and outbuildings. All abandoned. No doubt, Edwin and

Tara kept their equipment in there, or nearby.

As I worked through this, thinking, I caught Kingsley's amber stare. The brute wasn't even shivering, but his heart was hurting. I could see it in his anguished eyes. Yeah, he missed me. He also should have thought about that before breaking my heart.

Still, he had come all the way out here for me. So, I reached out and ran a hand over his beefy shoulder and said, "Thank you for coming."

"Anything for you, Samantha Moon," he said. "Anything."

I nodded sadly—perhaps for what could have been—and the three of us headed down the pine needle-covered dirt road that cut through the heart of the island, and headed north.

On a fool's run, no doubt.

43.

The storm seemed to be growing stronger.

Wind shrieked. Trees bent. Rain rattled leaves everywhere. As we trekked north, I couldn't help but think that Kingsley and Allison might be onto something. I was technically a carrier of one of the medallions, and my son...well, my son had *consumed* another medallion in a sort of potion concocted by one Archibald Maximus, who, as it turned out, was also quite the alchemist.

The medallion is in my son, too, I realized. *In his blood, perhaps.*

But what did the entity intend to do with my son? Was he going to drink from my boy? I shuddered and nearly worked myself into a panic. Jesus, and what did he intend to do with me? The medallion, as far as I was aware, was now eternally a part of me.

There were four such medallions, and if one of them was indeed hidden on the island, that would be three. The whereabouts of the fourth were unknown to me...and yet, even as I thought about that, the fleeting hint of a memory came to me. And then left just as quickly.

Good God, did I actually know where the fourth medallion was?

I didn't know, but I figured it was best to approach this one medallion at a time.

More importantly: what did the bastard want with all four medallions?

Allison, who'd been casting me sidelong glances in between cautiously stepping over exposed tree roots, also had been following my train of thought. Her words came clearly to me now as we stepped into an open area of the forest: *He mentioned releasing his sister, Sam.*

A sister who was presently trapped within me. A blessing and a curse, surely. A blessing because her dark power fueled my now-dead body, and, in turn, gave me superhuman abilities. A curse because I was now being used by her. I was, in effect, serving as her host.

I shuddered.

But how could the medallions help his sister break free? I asked.

Lordy, Sam, how would I know? Heck, just a few days ago I was a hair stylist/personal/trainer

/photographer/actor in Los Angeles.

That's a lot of slashes, I thought.

It's called "multiple streams of income." Oh, and you can add another slash.

Oh, yeah?

Private investigator assistant.

We'll see, I thought. *So, what good does it do us to find the medallion first?*

I don't know, Sam, but it might give us some leverage. In the least, it could thwart his nefarious plan.

I almost laughed at her word choice. Truth was, any plan that involved harming my son was nefarious. As we continued on, I wondered again how the medallions could be of use to the entity. After all, weren't the golden discs inherently good? They were, after all, created to counteract the effects of vampirism.

Unless, Allison said telepathically, *all four medallions come together. Perhaps then they can be used for evil. After all, a gun can be used to either defend or to murder.*

I looked at her. "That was shockingly erudite," I said.

"I have my moments," she beamed.

"What're you two talking about?" asked Kingsley, pausing and looking back. His long hair flung water everywhere, not that it mattered. We were in the open again and rain was literally driving directly into our faces.

"Girl talk," I said sweetly.

"Fine," he said irritably. "Looks like we're here."

Indeed, I could now hear the pounding of the surf, of water exploding against rocks. The hiss of retreating foam. We were at the north end of the island, near what appeared to be a straight drop down into the ocean below. Yes, the ocean was angry. The rain was angry.

Hell, even I was a little angry.

No, I was a *lot* angry.

"Okay," I said, "let's find this goddamned medallion."

44.

We stood at the cliffs.

My jacket flapped crazily. My jeans were soaked through. Yet, I never felt so alive. Wind and rain were elemental. I often felt elemental, too, deeply connected to the rhythms of night and day.

Allison, on the other hand, looked miserable. Her cheeks could have been two freshly-picked cherry tomatoes. She had also started sneezing. I needed to get my friend out of the storm—but to where, I didn't yet know.

"Where to, Sam?" Kingsley asked on cue. He seemed to be enjoying himself. This was the first time I'd seen the big gorilla since the 'incident.' If anything, he looked even sexier. Dammit. Apparently, wet clothing suited him well. I loved a man with meat on him, and Kingsley had just that. Thick and meaty equaled great cuddling.

"Don't know," I said, although my voice might have been lost on the howling wind.

The evening was coming on full dark—although never too dark for me. The ocean was alive to my eyes, foaming and frothing and churning. Salt spray exploded from below with each crashing wave. Some of that salt spray reached us. I tasted it on my lips, and then spat it out again.

I didn't know why I seemed to attract the medallions. Somehow, someway they seemed to find me.

He fearlessly stepped to the edge of the cliff and leaned out, looking down. Massive and immovable, he looked a bit like a cliff himself, only hairier.

"You said some others have been digging for it, too?" asked Kingsley.

I caught his meaning. "You think we should start where they've been looking?"

"It's not a bad idea. After all, they might have narrowed things down for us."

"Except I don't know where they've been digging—"

"I heard someone mention some caves that were near the beach," said Allison, cutting me off. "If I were shipwrecked and wanted to hide my gold, that's where I would pick."

From here, I could see a wide swath of sand not too far away, where the cliff dropped down to meet the beach. Which is where Allison suddenly set off for, sneezing as she went.

"I guess we follow her," said Kingsley, chuckling lightly. He bowed in my direction and waved his hand. "After you, madam."

We followed Allison down the grassy slope, slogging through puddles and ducking against the wind. My new friend seemed oddly determined. And her mind, perhaps even more oddly, was closed off to me.

I frowned at that as I followed her, as Kingsley's sasquatch-like footfalls crashed through the tall grass behind me.

45.

Miraculously, Allison led us directly to a cave.

The opening was just far enough back from the shoreline to not be flooded, and yet still deep enough to provide shelter from the pounding rain. Once inside, as our breaths echoed—well, Kingsley's and Allison's breaths echoed—I pulled down my hood and asked Allison if she was doing okay.

"Just cold," she said. She smiled at me faintly, her mind still closed off.

To me, she looked...distracted. And was blinking far too much. Perhaps she'd caught a cold.

Perhaps.

It was then that my inner alarm began sounding...as always a steady buzz just inside my ear. I looked again at Allison and she again smiled sweetly at me.

"Well, now what?" asked Kingsley, hands on his hips and dripping everywhere. His big cartoon feet were buried in the soft sand inside the tunnel.

"Here," said Allison, pointing. She'd brought her cell phone and was now using its flashlight app.

I didn't need a smart phone flashlight app to see in the dark, and neither did Kingsley, but we were polite enough. She aimed the light toward the back of the deep cave, and revealed something that none of us were too surprised to see: digging tools. Shovels and picks and strainers. It looked like a looter's hangout.

Rocks were piled up back there, too, many of which had been moved. Yes, someone was looking for something here, and, by all appearances, had been doing so for quite some time.

Kingsley inspected the area with Allison. I didn't. Instead, I closed my eyes and did my best to block out their voices, which seemed to echo everywhere at once. I kept my eyes closed and turned in a small circle. I lowered my hands and opened my palms. I breathed deeply, slowly, focusing.

Focusing...

Focusing on the medallion, as if it existed, as if it really could be here in the tunnel.

I didn't know how to find something that was hidden. After all, I'd only stumbled upon the second medallion in old Charlie's mobile home quite by accident. Back then, I had closed my eyes, like I was doing now, and the medallion just appeared to me, without effort—

I gasped.

There it was.

Burning in my mind's eye.

Clearly.

And it wasn't that far away.

Except, of course, it most certainly wasn't in the tunnel.

I opened my eyes and headed out of the cave... and toward the crashing surf.

46.

I looked out over the dark ocean.

Tiny filaments of light brought it all to life for me, illuminating what should have been complete blackness. I stood there at the edge of the foaming surf, which occasionally washed over my now-ruined sneakers. Since I was already soaked to the bone, I didn't bother removing my clothes, including my shoes.

Kingsley came up behind me. Amazingly, I could smell a combination of nice cologne and something musky. Something wolfish, no doubt. He placed a gentle hand on my shoulder.

"Is it out there?" he asked.

"Yes."

"How far?"

"Far enough that I need to swim."

"Where, exactly?"

"An underwater cave."

"Are you going to get it?"

"Yes."

"You need my help?"

"No."

"Do you love me?"

I opened my mouth, stunned by the question. Leave it to the expert litigator to drop a bomb on an unsuspecting witness up on a theoretical witness stand. "No," I said. "At least, not like I used to."

"You still love me, but differently?"

"Not now, Kingsley."

"Right, right. The medallion. So, what are you going to do?"

I looked back...and up at him. "I'm going for a swim."

Before I headed out into the water, I caught Allison watching me from the shadows of the cave. I was quite certain she was smiling. A big smile. A very big smile.

***

I stepped into the foaming surf, Asics and all.

I might be immortal. I might be cold to the touch. But that didn't mean I relished the idea of stepping into what appeared to be the coldest ocean ever.

"Think warm thoughts, Sam," called Kingsley

behind me. For some reason, he seemed to be enjoying this. *Asshole.* Then again, the big yeti had recently made his own journey across this very body of water.

If he can do it, I can do it.

And so I started running, splashing through the ankle-high water. Shortly, the water rose to my knees, and when it got to my thighs, I took a massive, instinctive breath and dove forward, under a coming wave. I stayed under, kicking hard, using my strong arms to propel myself under the raging ocean.

I continued on, just a few feet under the surface. The occasional wave still rocked me, but shortly, I was ten feet or more underwater. Soon, I was deeper than that. Far deeper. I kicked hard, pulling myself forward with powerful strokes. The sound of the waves crashing above receded, and soon I found myself in a place of silence. Complete and utter silence.

I liked that.

I held the image of the cave system in my mind's eye. Luckily for me, the incandescent flashes of light that only I could see were just as prevalent down in the deep. That didn't mean I could see far, granted. No, in fact, I could barely see a dozen or so feet in front of me.

Good enough.

I wasn't worried about sharks or killer whales or even mermaids. A merman might be damn interesting, and I briefly found myself wondering again if such creatures really did exist.

Hell, why not? *I* existed.

Life down here was not abundant...at least, not this close to shore. I did see silver fish that scattered before me. Once, I sensed a darker shape above me, but nothing that triggered my inner alarm system, and so I continued on...down into the deep.

Down, down.

And there it was...

A dark opening emerging through the dark waters. It could have been the maw of a great beast, waiting for something cute and curvy and stupid.

Stupid was right...

I plunged straight into the tunnel.

Anything could have been waiting in there.

Anything.

47.

I trusted my inner warning system.

For now, all appeared safe, and so I swam down through the wide tunnel, past scurrying crabs and smaller fish. I tore through swaying seaweed, and startled something big that could have been a grouper; that is, if I knew anything about fish, which I didn't.

Either way, it flicked its thick tail and shot past me.

Well, excuse me.

I continued down. The walls seemed alive, as various plant life clung to it, all moving and swaying in the currents. Beautiful, I supposed. But I wasn't here to admire the ocean's beauty. I was here to recover something seemingly lost forever.

Seemingly.

My kids were a distant memory. Kingsley was a distant memory. Russell Baker and his beautiful biceps were a distant memory. All that I knew was right before me: a cave, the cold water, the ocean depths. I did not think of idle things. What Tammy and Anthony were doing right now didn't cross my thoughts.

I only knew the tunnel. I continued into it, swimming quickly, pulling at the water, kicking the water, moving faster than, no doubt, most experienced divers. I was a superhuman immortal on land or sea, apparently.

The tunnel twisted and turned. At times, it grew wider. At other times, I was forced to pull myself through small openings. I doubted scuba divers had ventured this far. Scuba equipment was limited...and wouldn't fit through the many crawl spaces I was presently pulling myself through.

And still I swam, keeping the image of the medallion firmly in my thoughts. It was my beacon...and I knew exactly where that sucker was.

I plunged into a small opening, not so small that I had to pull myself through this time, but small enough that I aimed my hands in front of me and brought my legs together. I was a mommy-shaped torpedo, plunging through the black water.

Black water that was alive to me.

Blazing with light.

I emerged into a massive underwater cavity. A cavern perhaps, but filled completely with water.

That someone could have been here before me was an amazing concept. But someone had.

Another immortal.

The Librarian. The alchemist.

I swam down to a grouping of smaller rocks and saw the satchel there, swaying in the currents. How a satchel could have survived so long in salt water was beyond me. Then again, much of what the Librarian could do was beyond me.

I grabbed the bag, paused briefly, then turned, kicking hard, and shot up through the water, up through the tunnel and then, after an indeterminate amount of time, surfaced far from shore.

I saw Kingsley waiting anxiously near the crashing surf.

Holding the satchel, I grinned and began swimming for the beach.

48.

We were back in the tunnel.

I wasn't shivering, although I should have been. Then again, I should have been dead somewhere deep inside that tunnel system, too. But I wasn't, of course.

The freak lives on.

Allison crowded me eagerly, her mind still closed off to me. Did she know her mind was closed off to me? I didn't know, but would talk to her about it later.

Kingsley, admittedly, took up most of the tunnel. A ceiling that I had thought was high actually got brushed by his big head.

The satchel sat dripping on a rock before us. The bag itself had been leather at some point, but was now black and seemed to be deteriorating with each passing minute.

Perhaps it had been held together by alchemical means.

Waiting just for me.

Perhaps.

I looked at my friends. Kingsley nodded. Allison's eyes were alight with an inner fire. Then I began opening the bag. And by the time I'd done so, the material irreparably fell away in tatters.

Revealing a single coin.

Not a coin, actually. A golden medallion inlaid with three opal roses. It caught the light of Allison's silly flashlight app, refracting it beautifully.

That such a medallion was presently in me was hard to fathom. That my son had consumed one in a potion was another hard reality to accept. That a demented entity was bent on releasing his trapped sister within me, was, of course, the hardest to believe of all.

But it was all true.

Every bit of it.

Further proof that I was undoubtedly in an insane asylum, far away from here, rambling to myself incoherently while nurses and staff stared at me sadly.

Perhaps, perhaps not.

For now, I was standing in a mostly-dry cave, staring down at the third of four priceless medallions. Priceless, that is, to me and my kind.

The vampire kind.

"Well, now we know why the others couldn't find the medallion," said Kingsley. "It was meant for you to find, Sam." He held my gaze. "You and only you."

I nodded. Of that I had no doubt. Except how and why Archibald Maximus knew I would be here 100 years later was, of course, the greater mystery.

"The first medallion reversed your son's vampirism," said Kingsley.

"Mostly," I said.

He nodded. He knew all about my son. No, we hadn't been romantic over these past few months, but we had kept in touch, and I had consulted with him on Anthony's growing powers.

"And the second one..." he began.

"The second helps me exist in daylight."

"So, one has to wonder," said Kingsley. "What will the third one do?"

"A good question," said Allison, who had remained silent up until now. "But one that must, sadly, go answered."

I turned to her, frowning. God, she'd been acting so weird...

And then I saw it...what had been a miniscule black thread, so tiny that it had gone unnoticed by me, quickly swelled before my eyes. I had a brief image of a garden hose coming to life, engorged with water, swelling, thickening.

The black, ethereal ropes encircled her aura, weaving in and out. Lariats of death. It was as if Satan himself had lassoed my friend.

Her dark eyes, once beautiful and full of sweet mischief, now shone with fear—even while her lips curled into a Cheshire cat-like smile, the corners of her lips pushing up deeply into her rounded cheekbones.

"Is your, um, friend okay?" asked Kingsley.

"She's fine," answered Allison, in a voice I now recognized, its inflection similar to what had come from Edwin and Tara. And now from Allison. "She's just sort of taking, let's say, a temporary back seat."

"Sam..." said Kingsley, now facing Allison. "What the devil is going on?"

"He's here," I said. "In Allison, except I don't..."

"You don't understand how, Samantha Moon? Perhaps some things you aren't meant to understand, my dear. But let's just say this: your friend was right, she is indeed *distantly* related to the Thurman clan."

I grabbed the medallion and backed away. I had no idea what the entity within could do, what sort of powers it possessed. But if it was truly a highly evolved dark master then it might be capable of anything.

"There is no escape, Samantha Moon," said Allison. Or, rather, said the entity within her.

I looked at the hulking Kingsley next to me. "I like our chances," I said.

"Surely you wouldn't hurt your friend, Samantha Moon," it said. Tears appeared in

Allison's horror-filled eyes, and poured down her cheeks.

"Just give me the medallion, Samantha Moon, and I will release your friend."

"Don't do it, Sam," said Kingsley.

"Or would you prefer to watch your friend drown herself in the ocean? Or, even better, bite off her own tongue and bleed to death in front of you?"

Allison's eyes widened, and I might have—*might have*—detected her shaking her head no. She was fighting the entity, I was sure of it, and one thing I was also sure of: she didn't want me to give it the medallion. I suspected I knew her reasoning: for now, the entity needed her alive. For now, she was safe.

"Why do you want my son?" I asked suddenly.

"I think you know why we want your son, Samantha Moon."

I took a threatening step toward Allison—my sweet and silly friend Allison. The entity only grinned broader, which seemed impossible to do, but it somehow managed to pull the corners of her lips even higher up. Tears continued pouring from Allison's pleading eyes.

"Would you like to strike me, Samantha? If so, I *strongly* encourage it." The entity turned Allison's face toward me and chuckled lightly. "As the good book says, turn thy other cheek and all that."

"You're evil."

"I am *motivated*, Samantha, by that which is important to me."

"You want to release your sister," I said. "From me."

"That, my dear, is a very, very strong motivation."

"And you need the four medallions to do it."

It nodded, raising Allison's eyebrows. "I see you have done your homework, Samantha Moon. You never cease to impress us."

"I have one such medallion in me, and my son has the other in him. I'm holding the third. Where is the fourth?"

Allison turned to face me. Kingsley, I noted, had moved close to my side. He was ready to pounce at a moment's notice. Kingsley might be a womanizing bastard, but he was certainly all hero.

The entity continued regarding me through Allison's eyes. "I see you do not remember, Samantha."

"I don't have any idea what you're talking about..."

"Sssister," hissed Allison. "Speak to her, remind her of what she has seen and forgotten."

I knew instantly of whom he spoke: the female entity within me. *His* sister. Even as I shuddered, a memory materialized within me, summoned, I suspected, by the dark entity who shared my body.

It was an image of Fang.

I gasped, and Allison grinned.

The image clarified, took on more shape. It was an image of Fang back before I knew he was Fang, back when he was just a flirty bartender. He always gave me and my sister so much attention—and now I knew why, of course. He'd stalked me, relentlessly. He'd also fallen in love with me. So many emotions with Fang: from anger to love to everything in between.

The image clarified further...the longish teeth that hung from his chain...teeth that I had once falsely assumed were shark teeth. They weren't, of course. They were *his* teeth, pulled cruelly in an insane asylum...pulled from his very mouth.

The image clarified further still. It was Fang smiling broadly at me and my sister, leaning an elbow on the scarred counter at Hero's in Fullerton.

There was something on his chest.

Just behind the fangs that hung from the leather strap.

Was it a tattoo?

No.

The image clarified further, coming into even sharper focus.

It was a circular-shaped pendant hanging from his neck. But I hadn't recognized it because it had been flipped over, revealing only its golden backside.

The fourth medallion?

"Fang," I whispered.

Allison grinned broadly, even as her eyes pleaded for me to help her. "Ah, sssister. I see she remembers now. The fourth medallion is, in fact, not very far at all."

"Sam..." said Kingsley next to me, pulling me

out of my reverie. "Sam, you might want to see this..."

I blinked and looked to where he was pointing.

Through the cave opening, I saw people coming. Slowly, deliberately, plodding through the sand along the beach. Toward the cave. Toward us.

I recognized them all.

The Thurmans. From the very old, to the very young, a dozen of them or more.

Sweet Jesus.

I snapped my head around and looked at Allison. The entity within her tilted her head slightly. "We are legion, Samantha Moon, and we will have the medallion—*all* of the medallions."

49.

"We can't hurt them," I said. "They're innocent."

"They might be innocent," said Kingsley grimly, "but they look like they mean business."

They also looked like zombies. Already many of them were appearing at the cave entrance, compelled by forces they might not have entirely understood.

Edwin was there, and so were his many cousins. There was Tara, too, just behind him. Old and young, all the Thurmans looked confused. Most were shivering from the cold, drenched, unprepared for the weather.

The dark cords that bound them—that cursed

them—were all engorged, filled with hate, with venom. The cords pulsated and rotated and twisted through their otherwise beautiful auras.

Somehow, the entity had possessed them all, simultaneously—and it was a heinous, horrible thing to see.

In that instant, Edwin charged, baring his teeth, dashing supernaturally fast through the short tunnel. Kingsley leaped in front of me and, with one mighty swipe of his meaty arm, sent Edwin flying hard into the stone wall to our side.

A dull thud...and now Edwin was slumping to the ground, bleeding from a head wound. He was alive, but unconscious.

Kingsley looked at him only briefly, and immediately turned his attention to an older gentleman, an uncle, who next made his own charge. The result was similar, although Kingsley, I noted, didn't hit the guy quite so hard.

"They're stronger than they look," said the werewolf.

"It's him," I said. "*He's* making them stronger."

Kingsley nodded as the older gentleman shook his head and picked himself up. I suspected that if all of the Thurmans attacked at once, things would to get very ugly. "Are you sure we didn't step onto the set of a George Romero movie?" he asked.

"Sadly, no," I said.

"I think," said Kingsley, surveying the bizarre group before us, "something else is controlling them, from afar."

"Why do you say that?"

Kingsley reached back for me and took hold of my hand. "Who brought this curse upon the family?"

"Conner Thurman," I said. "Ninety years ago."

"We need to find him, Sam."

"He died," I said. "A long time ago."

Kingsley looked back at me and, amazingly, gave me a sardonic smile. "That," he said. "I seriously doubt. Trust me on this, Sam. I've seen some weird shit in my time. Granted, the walking dead is about as weird as it gets. But a curse like this needs a primary source. A head, so to speak. And that source—or head—would be Conner Thurman himself."

"He's entombed in the family mausoleum," I said. "Here on the island."

"Find him," said Kingsley, squeezing my hand. "And cut off the head of the snake. And I don't mean that figuratively."

"Jesus," I said.

"Pray all you want, but until Conner Thurman is found and destroyed, this curse will never, ever end —and they will never, ever stop coming for you and your son."

I thought about that as the Thurmans converged together. It was definitely about to get very ugly in the cave.

"I can hold them off, Sam," Kingsley said over his shoulder. "I can do so a lot easier and safer for them if I don't have to worry about you, too."

"But—"

"Go, Sam. Now!"

50.

As a male cousin dashed forward, sprinting supernaturally fast, Kingsley met him. This fight was more even, and Kingsley, I saw, had his hands full.

"Go, Sam!" growled Kingsley, finally heaving the young man off him, just as another sprinted forward. "Go now!"

I went, sprinting quickly through a gap between the Thurmans. Two peeled off and gave chase, while the others converged on Kingsley. Allison, to my dismay, was now running swiftly behind me.

Unbelievable.

But they weren't quite as fast as me. I suspected this was because the entity's own great strength was spread among many, rather than focused on one.

When I looked back again, I saw that I was alone in the forest.

The storm, amazingly, had subsided somewhat, although thick drops still splattered against my face. The medallion was also still clutched tightly in my hand.

I thought of Allison as I ran. The entity had threatened to kill her. Could he kill her? I recalled the shadow that had risen up in Cal, the shadow that had strangled the life out of him.

Yeah, I thought. *The entity could kill her.*

I picked up my speed.

Trees swept by in a blur. Once, I tripped over an exposed root and tumbled, my momentum carrying me many dozens of yards over the moist forest floor. I scrambled to my feet, aware that my right arm was broken at the wrist. A helluva tumble.

The pain was intense, but brief. I held my arm to my side and picked up my pace, and by the time I was at full speed again, I was certain my arm had healed completely.

So weird.

I flexed my hand as I ran, and the last of the pain subsided.

So very weird.

The dirt road soon opened into the Thurman's back yard. The manor beyond was brilliantly lit—and noticeably empty. Patricia Thurman was in there somewhere...and anyone else not blood-related. Undoubtedly, she would be wondering what the hell was going on.

And I thought my family was weird.

Far behind me, I heard the sound of running footsteps. Allison and another person were still behind me, following.

I paused briefly, then hung a right and headed for the massive stone edifice that stood adjacent to the property, and was surrounded by a thin band of trees.

The Thurman Mausoleum.

51.

The mausoleum looked creepy, even to a vampire.

Admittedly, I didn't know what the hell I was doing, or what, exactly, I was looking for. Yet, Kingsley had made a good point: destroy the man responsible for all of this insanity.

That was, of course, if the man responsible was still alive.

Official death records had reported the man's death decades ago.

I tended to not question official death records.

That is, of course, until my attack seven years ago. Now, I supposed, anything was possible.

The mausoleum was situated about two hundred feet away from the main home, and was surrounded by a thick row of evergreens. Still, who would even want a mausoleum so close to a family vacation home?

I didn't know, but it was perhaps someone who needed to keep an eye on the mausoleum. Or, rather, someone in the mausoleum who needed to keep an eye on the family.

Or both.

I shook my head at the insanity of it all.

Insane or not, the threat to Anthony and myself was real. And any threat to my kids was going to get my full and unwavering attention.

The mausoleum was composed of cement and plaster, its portico supported by two intricately carved Corinthian columns. Three broad stairs led up to what I imagined was a heavy front door and was, once I checked, locked.

I briefly wondered how Kingsley was faring against the Thurman clan. I could only hope they'd lost interest in him once they saw that I was gone. Either way, I was certain the big fellow could take care of himself.

Somewhere out there, crashing through the forest, was my friend Allison. My new and very close friend, who was, amazingly, distantly related to the Thurmans.

Go figure, I thought, and raised my foot.

I wasn't sure how heavy or thick the metal door was, but decided to kick with all my strength.

Which I did now, slamming it as hard as I could just under the brass door handle. The door didn't swing wildly open, and the handle didn't explode off the hinges, either.

But something cracked and the door moved.

I kicked again, perhaps even harder, and this time, the door did swing open.

I stepped through the doorway.

52.

I was here on a hunch.

Kingsley's hunch, actually. He believed that the entity was primarily focused through Conner Thurman. His theory did make a kind of sense. After all, my body was immortal, impervious to death, pain, or decay. All thanks to the dark entity within me.

Thanks to *her*.

So why wouldn't Conner Thurman, who originally summoned the entity nearly a century ago, also benefit from the dark presence within him? Yes, the more I thought about it, the more I was certain that he hadn't died.

Conner Thurman had been, of course, in the public eye. Had he been alive today, he would have been, what—I did some quick math, which was, of course, never my strong suit—and figured him to be around 125 years old.

He'd faked his death.

I was suddenly sure of it.

Yes, it felt right. Kingsley's hunch felt right. Long ago, a channeled presence had told me to trust my gut instincts. Trust my feelings. I might be able to do many things, but I could not predict the future.

Not yet, anyway.

Yes, I'd had a few prophetic dreams of late. Dreams where I could, in fact, see the future.

But this wasn't a dream. At least, I didn't think it was.

These days, dreaming and reality often blurred. So much so that I continuously questioned my own reality. The only constant was my love for my kids. They were my rock. My safety net. My love for them was more real than anything. It transcended everything. All the craziness.

If not for them...I would have descended, I was certain, into complete madness.

I held it together for them.

But now, someone was threatening my son.

I clenched my fists and stepped deeper into what was, in fact, my first mausoleum. It was cold, yes. Dark, yes. No windows. Correction, two stained glass windows situated high above. The floor was a highly polished marble, now made slippery by my soaking-wet Asics.

Hunch or not, one thing was for certain: my

inner alarm was ringing loud and clear.

Here be danger.

I was in a sort of long hallway with a high ceiling. On either side were shelves of some sort. The walls and shelves were composed of the same marble as the floor. Along some of the shelves were vases and flowers. Spaced along the walls were various plaques, all depicting names and dates of births and deaths.

My footsteps squished. Water dripped from me. I wasn't breathing, and so there was no echo of breath.

The tomb was silent.

Or should have been.

I cocked my head, listening in the dead of night.

Yes, there was a sound from somewhere.

Footsteps.

I paused, and verified the footsteps were not my own. Indeed, they continued on, echoing within what sounded like a stairwell. My hearing was good, granted, and the acoustics of the tomb enhanced the sound wonderfully.

Someone, somewhere, was coming up a flight of stairs. I was sure of it.

A flight of stairs that were directly ahead of me.

I remained motionless. I felt my normally sluggish heart pick up its pace.

Directly ahead of me, further down the narrow hall, a shaft of light suddenly appeared as a door opened.

Despite myself, I gasped.

A figure stepped out.

A figure I immediately recognized, at least from the pictures I'd seen. Conner Thurman. He looked remarkably good for being 125 years old.

I was careful to guard my thoughts.

"I see you found my home away from home, Samantha Moon," said a clipped and cultured voice. "Or, rather, my home *next* to my home." He chuckled lightly.

"You live here?" I asked, finally finding my voice.

"Often, although I get out as well, generally in disguise. But, yes, you could say that this is my sort of home base."

Was I talking to Conner Thurman or the entity within? I didn't know. Perhaps a little of both. Conner was a tall man who appeared to be in his mid-forties—likely the age when he had first been possessed by the entity within.

I noted he was not smiling, not like the others. Also, I couldn't see his aura, nor read his mind. He was completely closed off to me. Like Kingsley, or Detective Hanner, or the other immortals I'd encountered.

Yes, I thought. *He is the source.*

The source of the curse.

His family's curse.

Also, I was certain that Conner Thurman—the real Conner Thurman—had been overtaken completely by the entity within. Where the real Conner Thurman was, I didn't know, but I suspected he was trapped within, watching helpless within his own body.

Similar to the way the entity within me watched from within my body. Trapped within me—and wanting out. To possess me fully, similar to the way the entity now fully possessed Conner Thurman.

"Who are you?" I asked. I was aware of movement outside the mausoleum. I suspected Allison and perhaps some others had arrived. For now, they stayed outside. Undoubtedly, they were being controlled by the entity before me.

"I am a renegade of sorts, Samantha Moon."

"What do you mean?"

"You could say I don't play by the rules. I create my own rules."

"What rules?"

"The rules of life, death and our immortal souls."

"I don't understand."

"I, and my sister within you, have challenged the powers that be, so to speak. Successfully, I might add. We have effectively removed ourselves from the soul's evolutionary process."

"I don't understand."

"Yes, I'm sure you don't. You see, there are universal laws in place that govern not only this world, but the worlds beyond. Others before you have created these laws, laws that govern your soul's journey through life and death. I happen to not agree with these laws, Sam. I happen to have a rather rebellious streak within me. You see, I like to do things my way. And so does my sister, and so do many others like me."

He began circling around me, hands clasped behind his back. He went on, "You see, we have figured a way out of this rat trap, Samantha Moon. And you can join us. Forever join us."

"What do you mean?"

"Give my sister the freedom she seeks, and you can share in our eternal journey."

"And if I refuse?"

"There is no refusing, my dear. You will become one of us or nothing."

I found myself backing away. There was the scent of something repugnant wafting off him. An actual smell of decay, perhaps. My inner alarm seemed to be blaring off the hook. Yes, I was in serious danger, I got it. I willed my own alarm to quiet down. Sometimes, the damn thing went off so loud that I couldn't hear myself think.

"You killed George Thurman and Cal Thurman."

"Yes, I kill when my hosts become problematic or useless."

"What will you do with my son?" I asked.

Conner Thurman stopped pacing and faced me. "Unfortunately, Samantha, your son consumed something very important to me. Something very important to the process of releasing my sister. But not all is lost."

"What do you mean?"

"I'm sure you have figured out by now that I

will need all four of the medallions to release my sister."

I said nothing, already suspecting where this was leading. I clenched my fists.

"You see, I had a willing host. My host—Conner Thurman—permitted me to take possession of his body. And I gladly did so. Oh, yes. My sister's release requires aid, if you will. That's where the medallions come in."

"But why the medallions? I don't understand."

"The medallions were created to aid those like you, Samantha Moon. The combination of all four together was not foreseen, and not predicted. At least, not by those who created them."

He stepped closer, and I stepped back. I sensed great strength within him. I suddenly very much wished that Kingsley was by my side again.

"Fortunately, the magicks contained within the particular medallion that your son consumed are not lost."

"I don't understand—"

"Yes, you do, Samantha Moon. You understand all too well."

In a blink of an eye, he was behind me, reaching around my throat, one hand clawing up inside my sweater. I struggled but was shocked by his strength, his speed.

So strong, so fast.

His hand continued up over my stomach, over my breasts, up near my throat.

"You see, your son must now..." he began,

whispering harshly in my ear, his fingertips now pressing into the flesh of my upper chest, "be consumed completely and totally. Every inch of him. Every drop of blood. Every hair on his head." He was breathing harder, faster. "And trust me, Samantha Moon—trust me when I tell you that I will enjoy him very, very much. But first—"

I screamed, and not necessarily out of fear or anger, but because his fingers had dug deep into me. He threw me away as an excruciating pain ripped through me.

Stumbling into the hallway wall, I gripped my chest as blood poured between my fingers.

I looked back in horror as Conner Thurman held in one of his hands the medallion that had recently been under my skin, a medallion that was, even now, draped in my own bloodied flesh.

"One medallion down," he said, turning to face me, "and three to go."

53.

"Lucky for you, Samantha Moon, that I need to keep you alive. You are, after all, graciously hosting my sister."

I braced myself against the polished wall, even while blood from my chest continued pouring free.

"This may sound, ah, rather ghoulish, my dear, but all that precious blood of yours will not go to waste. I will have one of my—for want of a better word—Thurman minions gather it up carefully for me later. Waste not, want not." He laughed.

The pumping blood quickly slowed to a dribble. I could literally feel the wound closing underneath my palm.

I gasped and stood straight.

He pointed to the disc-shape bulge in my front

pocket. "It would be so much easier, Samantha, if you would just give me medallion number two."

"Fuck you."

"For some reason, I thought you would say that." He cocked his head to one side. "Forgive me, sssister," he said, the word hissing from between his lips. "For what I am about to do."

He leaped forward so fast that I had only enough time to turn my head. Still, the blow sent me spinning, and rocked me unlike anything I'd felt before.

And it had only been a partial blow.

I searched for the wall, couldn't find it, stumbled and fell.

He ran up to me, and in one smooth and horrible motion, kicked me full-force in the ribs, hard enough to lift me off the ground and hurl me deeper into the hallway, where I tumbled two or three more times.

I tried to gasp, but couldn't. Shards of rib bone had punctured my lungs. I was bleeding internally, and badly.

"My sister and I have decided that, perhaps, it would be best to keep you down here with me, Sammie. Oh, does it surprise you that I am still in communication with my sister? Oh, it's easy enough. She's accessible to me through your dream state. So, yes, we have prepared a special place for you down here, beneath my family's mausoleum. With the dead."

He came up to me and, if possible, kicked me

even harder, a blow that sent me crashing into the far wall and succeeded, I was certain, in breaking all of my remaining ribs. Blood poured from my mouth, from internal injuries that no one had any right to survive from.

I couldn't think. I couldn't comprehend. I didn't know, entirely, what was happening anymore. The pain was so intense—and happening faster than my own body could repair itself.

"But you have proven to be particularly worrisome, Samantha Moon."

I tried absently to push him away but I was certain that my arm was broken as well. He grabbed me by my bloodied jacket and lifted me up to my feet.

"Let me explain the source of my worry," he said, and then threw me against the nearby hallway wall. My head hit hard enough for me to have briefly passed out. Just briefly. Already, I could feel him lifting me up again.

"I haven't quite figured out why you, of all people, seem stronger than all the others. Yes, my sister within is a particularly evolved dark master, but that doesn't explain it, either. Do you see my dilemma?"

He backhanded me so hard that I was certain my jaw broke.

"You seem to have developed talents that far outweigh the others. Why, Sam? Why?"

He dropped me to the ground, where I slumped into a bloody and broken heap.

"Yes, we need to keep you here where I can keep an eye on you, while we fetch your son. Or, as I refer to him, medallion number three."

He turned and faced me.

My thoughts were scattered, incoherent, shattered. I might have been having a form of a seizure. I couldn't think. I couldn't function. I could barely see.

And as he began walking toward me, to deliver a blow that I knew would either kill me or render me completely useless, something appeared in my thoughts.

A single flame.

54.

Within the flame was a creature that I knew all too well. A creature much bigger than me, and much more powerful. A creature who was, in fact, *also* me.

The creature seemed to be waiting impatiently, and as the blurred form of Conner Thurman prepared for his final blow, the creature in the flame rushed toward me.

Filling me. Taking over me.

Becoming me.

***

The transformation was nearly instant.

My clothes burst from my body as I rapidly

grew and contorted. Soon, I was something that didn't belong in this world, nor any world, stronger and bigger than I had any right to be.

In a blink, my left hand reached out and grabbed Conner Thurman around the throat. He tried to speak, but only a strangled gasp emerged.

I lifted him off the ground, still holding him by the neck. I was tall enough now that my hunched shoulder just missed the stained glass windows high above. In fact, I very nearly filled the entire hallway. My leathery wings hung behind me.

I thought of the threats against my son.

I thought of what Kingsley had said to me:

Cut off the head of the snake.

And as I lifted him off the ground, as he kicked and gurgled and fought me, I continued squeezing.

And squeezing...

Something black and horrible appeared from his open mouth. A serpent, the same snake I had seen coiled around all of the Thurmans. It continued pouring out of Conner Thurman's mouth as if vomited by the Devil himself. Now it hung suspended in the air, twisting and coiling before me.

"Sssister," it hissed, and slowly faded away.

I growled and threw Conner Thurman hard against the far wall, and as he slid down, I swiped a massive claw cleanly through his neck.

55.

There were four of us in the library.

Allison was holding Tara's hand. The two of them sat closely together, sharing, perhaps, the world's most unusual bond: both had been possessed simultaneously by a nasty son of a bitch.

Kingsley occasionally patted my knee, and I let him. The gesture seemed to come from a source of support, not flirtation.

Earlier, I had called my sister and confirmed that they were all okay in a safe house. The safe house was, apparently, Kingsley's ski lodge in Arrowhead. I hadn't known Kingsley had a ski lodge in Arrowhead. Either way, all was well, and I breathed a sigh of relief and told them to sit tight for another day or so. I would explain it all later.

I had emerged from the mausoleum as naked as the day I was born and covered with blood—and completely healed. The headless body of Conner Thurman had done something extraordinary before my very eyes: it had literally gone up in smoke.

So weird, I thought now, as Kingsley patted my leg again. Tara cried softly as Allison hugged her close.

Allison had been outside the mausoleum, drenching wet and freezing and briefly confused. I helped her back to the bungalow where we changed into some dry clothes. Once done, she and I watched a very unusual procession: Thurman after Thurman emerged from the surrounding woods. All soaked to the bone. All lost. All confused. Some were even hurt. But none permanently so.

Kingsley emerged, too, carrying Edwin in his arms. The young Thurman had taken the worst of Kingsley's efforts to fend them off. Edwin, as far as I knew, was resting in his basement room now. Hurting, but okay.

Earlier, we had explained to Tara what had happened to her and her family. The news was, unsurprisingly, devastating. She looked at me now. "I hate him."

I waited. Outside, the storm had subsided. The trees were no longer threatening to break at their bases. A light rain drifted by the big windows.

"I hate him for what he did to my family. We couldn't fight him. We didn't know how. He manipulated our thoughts, our memories, our words, our actions. We were all his puppets."

I recalled the Source's words: *There is no evil, Samantha Moon.*

I wasn't sure I believed it. I had seen evil firsthand, and I believed it was real. I had seen the joy on the entity's face—or Conner Thurman's face—as it delivered blow after blow, breaking me and my body. A body that had, miraculously, been restored once I had transformed back into my human self.

Not even a cracked rib.

"You didn't know that Conner Thurman was still alive?" asked Kingsley.

She shook her head. "No, although the memories of serving him in the mausoleum are returning now..." she shuddered.

I didn't want to know what "serving him" entailed.

Sweet Jesus.

"He...he removed those memories from us."

Kingsley nodded. "He's gone now."

"I know," she said. "I felt him leave...and I felt him leave forever."

Allison was nodding. She looked at me and Kingsley. "I felt it, too. Granted, perhaps not as strongly as Tara, but suddenly, he was gone."

Tara nodded absently. I suspected she felt the same, except I knew the trauma of her ordeal ran so deep and for so long, that she would need many months or years to come to terms with what had happened to her and her family.

The Thurman family had a lot of healing to do. After all, did they really know each other? How much of their lives had been controlled by the entity?

I didn't know, but I did know that it was gone. I had seen it flee. To where, I didn't know. Perhaps another willing host. Perhaps even now it was cruising over the earthly plane like a diseased wind, looking for a willing partner...or perhaps even, an unwilling one.

Yes, I thought. *There is evil.*

The entity might be gone, but his sister was not. His sister was still within me, watching, waiting, existing. I shuddered all over again. Kingsley felt me shudder and patted me again. He added a small squeeze. Flirt.

Junior and Patricia Thurman next came into the room. Although Junior looked confused, he also looked vibrant. Noticeably absent—and perhaps most telling of all that the entity was indeed gone—was that his aura, along with Tara's and all the other Thurmans, was completely free of the black cord. The cursed black cord that had bound them all.

We left Tara with her uncle.

56.

I was back on Dome Rock.

The sun had not yet risen. Kingsley and Allison were asleep in the bungalow. It had been hours after the ordeal in the mausoleum.

God, had I really cut off his head?

I had. Or, rather, the thing that lived within me had.

No, it had been me. *I* had made a point to squeeze the life out of Conner Thurman—or the thing that animated Conner Thurman. I had made the decision to remove his head.

He'd *threatened* Anthony. He had been going to *kill* Anthony.

Consume Anthony, in fact.

Yes, I had cut off his head, and I would do so a

thousand more times if I had to.

The rain had finally dissipated. The ocean beyond seemed relatively calm. I could even see stars peeking through the thin cloud layer.

Before me were both medallions: the opal medallion that I had plucked from the ocean's depths, and the amethyst medallion that had once been embedded within my chest. Each glittered dully, catching whatever ambient light there was.

My chest had healed marvelously. Not even a scar.

"Penny for your thoughts," said a voice behind me.

I gasped, turning. I hadn't heard anyone approach, and my inner alarm had failed to notify me of danger. Standing behind was, of course, the young Librarian. The alchemist. He was wearing jeans and a sweater and shoes that didn't seem appropriate for a hike up Dome Rock.

"I'm sorry to startle you, Samantha Moon."

"How did you get here?"

"The ferries are running again."

"How did you know I was here?"

He smiled and walked around me and stood over the two medallions. "I, too, am intricately linked to these guys."

"Because you created them."

"Yes. Do you mind if I sit?"

"It's a big rock," I said.

He chuckled and sat before me. A small wind blew steadily over us. His short hair didn't move.

Neither did his clothing.

"There's some weird shit going on," I said.

"Yes, I imagine so."

"Why am I connected to the medallions?"

"I don't know, Sam, but I suspect it's a combination of many things."

"What things?"

"The vampire who first created you, for one. He was one of the oldest...and perhaps even one of the most powerful."

"I don't understand."

"Knowledge and power is always transferred through blood, Samantha. It is the carrier of all information, all knowledge. Have you not noticed that those around you, and those blood-related to you, are growing in power?"

"Yes."

"He infused you with his own knowledge, his own power. Sam, you have abilities you've not yet tapped into."

"I don't want them. I just want to be normal."

"That might still be possible."

I looked at him sharply. "What do you mean?"

He picked up the medallions. "I created these medallions, Samantha, to help someone like you find normalcy again."

"But they also do unspeakable harm," I said.

He nodded sadly. "There was an unforeseen consequence of the medallions, I'll admit."

"As long as they are in existence, my son will always be in danger."

"I cannot deny that, Sam. At least, if all four are in existence. However, they can also give back the normalcy you seek."

"So, my two choices are either normalcy for me or danger to my son."

He nodded once.

"That's not an acceptable option to me," I said.

"Then destroy one, Samantha Moon, and the medallions can never again be used for evil."

I nodded. I had been thinking the same thing. I touched the opal medallion. "What will this one do?" I asked.

"That one will remove your need to feast on blood."

"And the fourth medallion, the one that hangs from Fang's neck?"

Archibald Maximus, the young-looking guy with the old man's name, nodded. "Yes...the diamond medallion."

"What will it do?"

"A very interesting medallion, indeed."

I waited. Seagulls circled high above. Something small and undoubtedly furry scurried in the brush at the edge of the dome.

"If you'll recall, the ruby medallion reversed vampirism within your son."

I nodded. "Mostly."

He smiled. "The amethyst medallion gave you the ability to exist in the sun."

"Mostly."

"The opal medallion would remove your need

for blood."

"We'll see."

"The diamond medallion grants the user, in effect, *all three*."

"What do you mean?"

"Once the diamond medallion is invoked, Samantha, one would have all the powers of the vampire, without the shortcomings. One would, in effect, have it all."

"Immortality, too?" I asked.

He nodded. "And great power, great strength, everything you currently enjoy. Without that which you don't. It is, in effect, the answer to your prayers."

"Why make only one?" I asked.

He smiled sadly at me. "I only brought forth the medallions into the world, Samantha. Think of me as the potter. I did not create the clay, only the shape within. The energy was always here, waiting. I only gave it shape and form."

"Can you create more?"

"So far, no. But with intent, all things are possible."

"Meaning?"

"When something is wanted bad enough, the Universe answers the call."

"So, for now, all that exists are the four medallions?"

"Yes, one of which is now infused within your son."

"That sounds so weird," I said.

"Life is a little weird, Sam. Beautiful but weird."

"I cannot risk that another will come for me and my son," I said.

"I understand." He looked at me for a long moment. "You do understand that you can wear only one medallion."

I hadn't known that, but I did now. I nodded.

"You must choose one medallion, Sam."

I thought of my options, and I thought of Fang. "I want these medallions destroyed," I said.

He raised an eyebrow. "Both of them?"

"Yes."

"You are giving up the ability to go into the sun? To bypass the need for blood?"

"Yes," I said. "For now. Besides, the sun is overrated. I'm really more of a night person. And, honestly, who really needs Chicken McNuggets, right?"

"You're going to go after the fourth medallion," said Archibald.

"You bet your ass," I said.

He nodded.

"So, what do we do with these?" I asked, indicating the two medallions.

"It saddens the heart, but I shall destroy them. Admittedly, the harm they could cause was unforeseen."

"How will you destroy them?"

"How strong are you, Sam?"

"Stronger than I look."

He chuckled. "Of that I have no doubt. Yes, they are composed of gold and other alchemical materials. And like all alchemical artifacts, the spells within can be severed."

"You want me to break the spell."

"It has to be you, Sam."

Still sitting on the smooth rock, as the sky slowly began lightening, I reached over and picked up the amethyst medallion.

"You're sure about this, Sam? As soon as that medallion is broken, you will have only minutes to get back indoors. Your body will return to the day and night circadian rhythms of the vampire."

"I understand," I said. "For my son, I understand. And it's far too late to use such big words."

He chuckled lightly as I gripped the medallion in both hands.

And applied pressure. A lot of pressure.

Nothing happened at first—but then, suddenly, the medallion snapped in half, followed by what I was certain was a supernatural popping sound. Maximus winced slightly.

I did the same with the opal medallion, and soon four halves lay on the rock before me.

"It is done, Samantha Moon," said Maximus. "Would you mind if I took these with me," he said, indicating the four broken halves. "The metal is of use for other alchemical potions."

"Knock yourself out," I said. "But I do have one question."

"Just one?" he asked.

"Okay, many. Why did you hide the medallion so deep in the cave?"

"It was meant to be a test."

"A test?"

"Yes. The shipwreck was fortuitous in the sense that it gave me an opportunity to hide the medallion somewhere I'd previously not foreseen. Well, not entirely foreseen."

"And to the world it appeared that a treasure had gone down with the ship?"

"Right," he said.

"How would Conner Thurman know about the opal medallion?"

"Conner Thurman didn't. The entity within him did."

"Is that why they built this home on this island? To search for the medallion?"

"Part of the reason, I'm sure. Undoubtedly, they saw the seclusion here as a good thing, too."

"How was I able to find the medallion and he didn't?"

He smiled. "Because it was meant for you."

"I don't understand."

"Or, rather, it was meant for someone like you. Someone worthy. Someone strong. Someone who would bring some light into all of this craziness. Soon, Sam, dawn will break, and you no longer have protection from sunlight."

"Are you coming with me?" I asked.

"No, Sam. I prefer to sit here and watch the

sunrise."

"Don't rub it in," I said, slapping his knee.

He smiled sadly. "Go, Sam. You don't have much time."

Indeed, I could already feel my body shutting down with the coming of dawn. I got up and started moving across the domed rock. I looked back once and saw the Librarian now sitting cross-legged, his face lifted to the heavens.

Awaiting dawn.

For some reason, I found tears on my cheeks.

Not too long ago, I had seen my first dawn as a vampire. But now that ability was gone. It didn't have to be, of course. I could have chosen it. Or chosen the opal medallion—and never again have been forced to consume filthy blood.

Now, as I turned back to the trail that would lead down to the bungalows, to where Kingsley and Allison slept, I thought of Fang.

How he had found the fourth medallion, I didn't know.

Where he was, I didn't know.

But I was going to find him.

One way or another.

The End

About the Author:

J.R. Rain is an ex-private investigator who now writes full-time. He lives in a small house on a small island with his small dog, Sadie. Please visit him at www.jrrain.com.